VLADIMIR MAKANIN

BAIZE - COVERED TABLE WITH DECANTER

TRANSLATED FROM RUSSIAN BY

ARCH TAIT

READERS INTERNATIONAL

About the Translator: Arch Tait is the British editor of *Glas: New Russian Writing*, a journal published in Moscow and Birmingham, England. Dr Tait teaches Russian at Birmingham University and has translated numerous Russian writers, including Mark Kharitonov and Bulat Okudzhava who, like Vladimir Makanin, have been awarded the Russian Booker Prize for the Novel.

The title of this book in Russian is *Stol, pokrytyi suknom i s grafinom poseredine*, first published in *Znamia* (Moscow), No. 1, 1993. © Vladimir Makanin 1993

First published in English by Readers International, Inc., Columbia, Louisiana, and Readers International, London. Editorial inquiries to the London office at 8 Strathray Gardens, London NW3 4NY, England. US/Canadian inquiries to RI Book Service, PO Box 959, Columbia LA 71418-0959, USA. English translation © Readers International, Inc. 1995. All rights reserved.

The editors wish to thank the National Endowment for the Arts (Washington, DC) and the Arts Council of England for their support.

Cover illustration, 'A Complex Presentiment (Half-Length Figure in a Yellow Shirt), 1928-32' by Kazimir Malevich
Cover design by Jan Brychta
Printed and bound in Malta by Interprint Limited

Library of Congress Catalog Card Number: 95-74959
British Library Cataloguing-in-Publication Data: A catalog record for this book is available from the British Library.

ISBN 0-930523-66-0 Paperback

BAIZE - COVERED
TABLE
WITH DECANTER

Chapter 1

He is a bit of a drudge, but out of all of Them seated on the far side of the Table he is the first you notice. He seems to have been waiting for you ("Aaah, *there* you are..."). His eyes glint the instant you enter. He is thin, short, working class (no higher than technician), and he has a grudge against the rest of the world. Russia's history set his class instincts alight some time ago and they are still raging. To me he is the Proletarian Firebrand. In everyday life he is perfectly amicable, his name is Anikeev, he is an ordinary sort of chap but given to brooding. His bulbous wife goes off alone each year to a distant holiday resort and loses no time finding herself a fancy man there who is the spitting image of her husband, which makes it a puzzle why she bothers (unless to avoid too complete a break from routine). He harbours suspicions, resigns himself to accepting it as one of those things, flies into a rage, threatens murder, then tells himself he has imagined it all and is being over-possessive. His real gripe is how few good things have come his way. Everybody else seems to have fixed themselves up nicely by hook or (more often) by crook, even the newly appeared street traders (who are every bit as ignorant as he is). As for the intellectuals, they certainly haven't been slow off the mark since *perestroika.* What's going on? Aren't we in Russia all supposed to have equal shares? Well, aren't we? He grinds his teeth as he asks the question.

A bit of a drudge and a bit of a drunk, and with an expression of general goodwill hovering uncertainly about his face. No, he is not drunk today. Not a drop of vodka has gone down his throat. But yesterday or the day before he did hit the bottle and now and again, superimposing itself on that smile (almost welling up out of it), the day before yesterday's stoned look re-appears, and with it the aggression. Today it feels like spontaneous hostility, because although he did his drinking yesterday and the day before, it is only today, now, that he has found an enemy to focus on. Don't worry, he knows the rules. He's not about to bristle or rage at you. He's very controlled. For the moment there is no outward sign of his discovery. He just sits there slowly sucking in his cheeks and nailing you with his return glance, and thinking to himself, as yet undetectably:

"You smug bastard...!"

He is wearing a cheap but cheerful sweater, with the collar of a clean shirt showing at the neck. He has not shown up at the tribunal just any old way. These are serious matters. There are things here that need clearing up and straightening out, and it's all got to be above board. He peers sideways. Immediately to his left (from his viewpoint) and immediately to his right (from yours) sits the person who will ask most of the questions.

The One Who Asks the Questions sits almost at centre Table. He is another one you notice straightaway. As he asks his questions he seems to be flipping you not too roughly from side to side, not letting you get away, setting you up for the others. He is their tracker. (When you are being asked a question, you do not yet know yourself which way you are going to run. A hunted animal will run in circles, but how do human beings run when they are disoriented?) He does not probe too deeply with his questions: it is not his job. That is something for everyone to join in. But he is the master of the hunt. His unexpected questions (pointed, trivial) make you feel both that you are being hunted, and that you must try to hide from your pursuers.

"Well why could you not just have phoned us yourself, even in the evening, to let us know you were ill? By the way, what do you do in the evenings? Watch television? Football? See friends?"

There is no answering this question because there is no real question to answer, but you are sitting there saying nothing, not keeping up with him. You have not been shot down, but for some reason you don't understand yourself, you feel adrift and vulnerable, and your perfectly understandable bafflement opens up the ground for new questions. This is the territory he hunts in.

"So there is absolutely nobody you can phone in the evenings for a heart to heart talk? Have you always found yourself in this predicament?" he asks with a smile of disbelief, and again the question goes unanswered (and an insinuation is left hanging in the air. What sort of person are we dealing with here if he has never in his entire life managed to find a friend close enough for a heart to heart talk of an evening?) Another failure to answer, and again you register that you have been wrong-footed. So do those seated at the Table. Only the One Who

Asked the Question and gave them their first scent of blood seems not to have noticed anything. He carries right on, heading you up, slithering slightly as he corners and comes in from a completely different direction:

"Well, do you at least appreciate a woman for her personal qualities? I'm sure you treat her with proper respect..."

Again the unanswered insinuation: what kind of a weirdo do we have here? What sort of way has he been living his life all this time? This will come back to haunt you later on in one way or another. (Your having lost all sensitivity towards other people is not something they are going to let rest.)

The One Who Asks the Questions is an intellectual. He is dark, with smooth black hair and a fine, austere line to his cranium, emphasized by the way he turns his neck. He has his hands on the table, the long pleasing fingers intertwined with a languid nervousness not indicative of excessive temperament. He is a fast talker, firing questions, not bothered whether you smile or not, but smiling himself. Most likely a middle-echelon engineer in a research institute, and most likely he sometimes even checks over end results himself, tilting that cranium, its fine line emphasized by the way he turns his neck. He is not talkative but here, at the Table of judgement, he is animated and forceful, exerting himself not for his own good but for the good of society, the good of all of us. "What sort of person are you?" Another unanswerable question, but a question asked and not withdrawn, a door at which he is always the first to push.

Next to him sits the Secretarial Type, a man who seems always to be on the right side of middle age. He sits directly at the centre of the Table, opposite you. You are separated by the decanter, and you imagine he is going to have to peer round to the right or left of it if he wants to see you while asking a question. You turn out to be quite right (although he asks questions very rarely). Most of the time he is writing, setting down his notes on a piece of paper, ballpoint pen in hand. If somebody asks a question which you (and he) were not expecting, he looks expectantly at you not round the decanter but over the top of it. It is not a very tall decanter.

Glass tumblers are set out on the red baize tablecloth along the length of the Table, imparting a sense of unity to those seated at it and indeed to the picture as a whole. Sometimes bottles of mineral water stand assertively by the glasses, but the decanter stays there irrespective, binding the people and objects surrounding it. The presence of a geometrical centre unifies the Table, and gives the words and questions of those seated at it the force of an enquiry. It is just these attributes, simple as they may seem, which elevate your questioners to the status of inquisitors and oblige you to defer to them and feel threatened. And prepare yourself psychologically before you turn up, either to be brazen with them, or perhaps to take your tranquillizers. Imbibing hard liquor is inadvisable.

Everything interrelates. Their questioning may elicit that six months ago you were again fired from your job. (So?) They may discover that your son has now been married and divorced three times. (So?) They may call to mind that you tried to obtain false sick notes for your feckless offspring, that you got him registered for accommodation, registered for a residence permit, and subsequently re-registered. (So?) What is so threatening is that this is not a proper law court but a general quizzing all down the line in order to find something they can latch on to; to catch you out in some way, and then metaphorically but deftly nail your balls to the wall while you continue to sit there in silence, hanging your head in shame, repenting the fact of your existence, the fact that you eat and drink and evacuate your bowels while pretending to wash your hands. There is a personal side to it too. Everybody has grudges against life and peccadilloes that flow from them. Everybody has complicated, dodgy areas of their psyche, and simply the sharp corners of relationships; there are inevitable slippery patches in growing up emotionally, and there is all the general crap of daily living. If that is not enough, there are the pants you peed and pooped in when you were little. Everybody has a trail of torn shirts and soiled pants, the trash, the rubbish, the glitches and the garbage of everyday life and all of them, amazingly, prove interrelated as they are activated under the crossfire of their seemingly harmless questions. As if crushed by life's hectic interrelatedness, you rush to reply to their first, second, third, fifth, tenth question with deep personal commitment and overblown sincerity and a growing determination to answer more and more precisely and compellingly. And even more truthfully than the compromised truthfulness of the facts themselves admits as they leap suddenly out of your garbage-strewn, day-by-day existence to lodge in your conscious mind, and oblige it to justify them. It is unendurable, but with improbable patience you do endure it, and go on answering, answering, answering.

There are occasions, of course, when you march in to confront them with head held high. You snap right back at them aptly, wittily even. But your fine aplomb does not prove long-lived, and with every passing minute your fighting spirit leaks away under their quizzing like so much hot air out of a punctured balloon. The damage has not been done by their pinpricks. The hole was already there and has merely become evident as your hot air now dissipates through it. The puncture was there inside you, and try as you may to dissimulate you cannot now hide 'how you are feeling. They have only to drag out their sad hearing minute by minute and word by word, and watch you deflate until you are reduced to a shrivelled, empty, embarrassing skin. Worse, your confidence is now additionally undermined by embarrassment at the jauntiness, nay, the brazenness, of your entry. These, after all, are grown people who have assembled here and are voluntarily giving up their time to sit in this place, and then you come bouncing in without so much as a how's-your-father and start making a fool of yourself.

"He is being asked a question, and he sits there with his legs casually draped over each other..."

Or, slightly differently,

"Someone is speaking to him, and there he sits twiddling a pencil. Couldn't he have finished playing with that at home?!"

The voices suddenly come at you from several

directions at once. They have got the measure of you. They did not dare adopt that tone when you came in so aggressively, but now the voices come from all sides, giving no time to respond on the topic of yourself or the pencil you hold in your hands. You can only look from one face to another until finally there comes that shout, "Stand up!" or "Stand up when you're being spoken to!" as one of them goes over the top. The worst of it is, you do stand up. Before you have time to think you are on your feet and it is too late. The response to that shout and that voice is programmed into you. Having gone and stood up you may then realize what they have done and give them a piece of your mind. You may shout at them yourself, let slip your self-control and bawl them out hysterically. Indeed you may, but... you did, after all, stand up when told to. That is, after all, you standing now in front of them, shrieking, your lips twitching...

"But you do sometimes sit chatting with friends into the small hours, drink a little vodka of course, enjoy a joke with them, have a laugh?"

(The questioner really wanted me to be living a full-blooded life.)

"Not so often nowadays," I replied.

"You have a nice apartment and I'm sure now and again you feel like getting together with a few friends and people you know. Tell us about it. That interests us. All of us here want to get to know you better..."

He was smiling. They were all smiling. They wanted to know how exactly I lived this full-blooded life of mine (if in fact I did). They consider this the first fruit of their hearing: just finding out (for no particular reason) what makes some ordinary person tick, what he gets up to. They want to live his life with him in imagination.

"You sound as though you might have a good singing voice. Do you sing? When you're with friends, perhaps?"

"No."

They were disappointed.

"Come now. I am quite sure you do sing, and to a large circle of friends and family."

I shook my head negatively.

There was a long, blank pause. (For no reason whatsoever I had again lost face.) I asked, already wilting,

"Why, is that bad?"

They nodded, as if to say well yes, actually, it was rather a pity if that was how I lived my life. Guilt feelings washed over me. I remember thinking, "Why don't I just give up now? They are obviously right. I am guilty, and I would still be guilty if there were a whole choir of me singing the Hallelujah Chorus to my family and friends every evening in life."

Strictly speaking, only half the equation is really known in advance, and that is, that they are right. (This does not necessarily mean that you are in the wrong from the outset.) We are all only human, and that is why you are apprehensive that your shortcomings, from those pants dirtied in childhood to the drops of sweat on your brow as they ask their question ("What is it, actually, that you are worrying about right now?"), are somehow going to peep out and be caught in the limelight, even though they bear no relation to their questions (except that, as we know, everything interrelates). You aren't pleading guilty, you're just feeling guilty.

"We are all busy people," the voice on the telephone told me curtly (one evening). "You are not the only one. When it comes down to it, this is for your benefit not ours. You are the one needing the reference, the certificate about your wages, and the form detailing how and why you left your job. Quite apart from the fact that in five years or so you absolutely must have all these papers if you are to obtain your pension." (They really have that side of things wrapped up.) "That's why we are expecting you."

"You make yourself clear."

"We just need to sit down together and have a talk. There are a few things that need straightening out."

"All right, all right. I'll be there."

I had no sooner said it than I realized I should never have agreed. (They could have sorted it out some other way.) With my nerves and weak heart I can't afford to sit down in front of that Table covered in red baize. They have no business asking me to in my present state of health. (My blood pressure is already nearly 200, and there's the whole night to get through yet.)

"All right, all right. I'll be there." I even hurled the receiver down as if to say, "Bloody typical. Up yours!" Such heroism! The fact of the matter is that, for as long as I can remember, these sessions in front of the Table have brought me nothing but humiliation, only a feeling of having been run over by a steamroller (which, needless to say, is entirely my own fault).

"I don't need this. I'm not going," I tell myself; but of course I shall, if not at the first time of asking then at the third or the fifth. There is no getting away from them. (The rub is that the people seated at the Table are already like my own kin, part of my life. They know me backwards, as I do them. They get younger, the team changing year by year, while I remain the same; so that there is only one way for our protracted relationship to end: with my physical absence, my demise.

"Take it easy," my wife says.

"Uh-huh."

"Do you want supper? It's porridge. Yes, again. Yes, I know porridge is better in the morning, but the milk isn't fresh and we need to use it up."

We sit down to supper and call my daughter through. I don't want (I am ashamed) to admit that my nerves and anxiety are to do with tomorrow's summons, so I spin them some nonsense about a problem at work.

"Well, fine. Now just take it easy," my wife repeats.

Despite my efforts the conversation comes round to tomorrow's hearing, and I reluctantly tell them I am not at all looking forward to the prospect of those idiotic people prying into my private life. I may be able to fob them off, but they will still have fingered my soul. "Just put up with it," says my wife. We eat our supper. (The commission will convene, just for a talk and to establish one or two things. Exactly. To establish whether you are a decent human being or not. And while they are at it, whether you are a good husband and father, and whether you are a good resident on your staircase... What a trial, in more senses than one. You imagine this, that and the other to yourself, and when you go in you see that this is the same tribunal you have known since ever was, from your very earliest years. Handing on the baton to one another, they have spent the whole of your life trying to establish whether you are a decent human being, and still haven't managed to make up their minds.

"Oh, do stop grumbling," my daughter begs.

I sit in silence, and so do they, and we rhythmically dip our spoons in the bowls of porridge.

Trying to conceal my agitation seemed only to have made it worse. It's not the first time. I ought really to have taken a good dose of valerian. ("You have to anticipate," a doctor who once looked after me advised.) I ought to have taken some valerian and relaxed, but I told my wife and daughter I was very tired and just wanted to get to bed as soon as possible. It had been a hard day for all of us so they went along with me, and we retired to bed at eleven (or shortly before). At twelve I had a turn. Much belated swallowing of medicine, my blood pressure taken twice, and a quarrel over whether or not to call an ambulance. "This is really dangerous. You have no idea how dangerous it is," my daughter shouted, and even shook a finger at me. I shouted back. My wife was shaking. She ran from the telephone to me and from me back to the telephone. I think she was wanting to phone our son (he doesn't live with us). My heart was still misbehaving. I could feel the pressure building up, and then it would suddenly treacherously relax. The faces of my wife and daughter would blur as my head swam, and beyond them I could see blurred walls and a faraway window with blinds. "Just don't pop your clogs," I thought. The closeness of death was not frightening but so prosaically straightforward that I stopped arguing with them. I became very quiet.

I simply lay there, half closing my eyes, and told them softly,

"Go to bed. Let's go back to sleep."

I said it so matter-of-factly that they were persuaded. They went to bed, and shortly after both of them went back to sleep, my daughter first, and then my wife.

I lay prostrate. I now wanted less than ever to admit to myself (let alone my family) what was causing all this pain in my heart and general anxiety and alarums in the night.

I even dozed off. Some time after one in the morning I felt the tension coming on again, and an extra systole after every two heartbeats. I got up and sat on my couch with my bare feet hanging over the edge. Should I anticipate another turn?

I pushed on my slippers, went out into our narrow corridor, and padded soundlessly to the kitchen. It was dark. It was still. Outside the window (I looked out) it was dark too, houses asleep, roofs, dark empty balconies. *I must boil up some valerian root...* It suddenly occurred to me that this is just how life is, and I must have been summoned to "talks" like tomorrow's a hundred times before, if not two hundred. If not more. This petty quizzing had been going on for many long years, trivial but, just as now, niggling, unnerving, driving you to distraction. The penny suddenly dropped as I realized that the particular reason for calling you in is of no importance to your interrogators and never has been. They are concerned with something quite different. With this insight, I sat down (on a kitchen chair in the middle of the night) and, newly resigned, no longer cursing and swearing at myself, propped my head up in my hands and gave myself over to hurting inside with a pain which had stolen up on me.

Aaargh. Aaaaargh... several times.

The night wears on.

Sometimes when I am wandering along the corridor at night from our room to the kitchen and back again (sometimes sitting down on a kitchen chair for a bit), it seems to me that timing my steps to coincide with my heartbeats protects my heart. The rhythm of my footsteps is restful.

I do not want any more of her (my wife's) night flaps. I do not want to sense her alarm. I mooch around, pulling an old coat round me. (I don't wear a robe. I don't have one.) I pull it round me because I am feeling cold. I am not afraid as such, but it is as if we have a mutual agreement: fear does not look me in the face, nor I him (but he builds up somewhere inside, coming to the surface near the middle of my backbone, and I feel him as a chill). I keep walking around, doggedly trying to while the night away. I get a pill out in case my blood pressure shoots up and, of course, some nitroglycerine. I unhurriedly boil up the valerian root in the kitchen. (There are no valerian drops to be had. There is nothing in the pharmacy these days.) I prefer to look after myself. I find life simpler without sympathy. If my wife does get up she will see, just as she is coming out of sleep, a shambling creature in an overcoat with slippers on its bare feet, old and bent down by insomnia and worrying thoughts which follow on ceaselessly, one after the other. The eyes of this creature, which looks like a sick animal, will suddenly flash at her out of the darkness of the corridor, and only then will she recognize, admit that she recognizes me. She will, of course, immediately start feeling sorry for me and calming me down. I want none of that. It just burdens me even more. But before she gets round to calming me down and feeling sorry for me there will be that instant of surprise in the night, that bewilderment when she suddenly glimpses a stooping body with an old coat slipping off its shoulder (it lost its last buttons long ago), coming down the corridor from the direction of the kitchen, and realizes that this creature is her husband.

I remember an incident I had almost forgotten (which really was quite trivial). A year ago when the lines were enormous a fight broke out. I found myself standing too close to people who first shouted and then grappled with one another. Fists were soon flying, people being grabbed by the lapels. The police were on the scene as promptly as ever and, as ever, got the wrong end of the stick. They rounded up a dozen people, including me, with their customary indiscriminateness. Then it was, "All down to the police station, hands behind your backs, don't you worry, we'll soon get to the bottom of all this... You'll be free to go just as soon as we've had a look at your ID. What do you mean you haven't got your ID with you?" For some reason, however, the police did not deal with the matter themselves: they took the easy way out and booted the entire trawl over to the custodians of the public interest. "All of you to room such-and-such!" (Twenty-seven, I think it was.) "Move it, you mother-fuckers, Room 27!"

When I did go into room such-and-such, to the accompaniment of much noise and a chorus of shouting, I saw in there the oaken Table and the people seated at it, and straightaway I noticed a familiar civilian type, not too bright, something of a drudge perhaps, the Proletarian Firebrand, his face not yet twisted into hostility (but ready to be). He looked me over and murmured, so far amicably enough,

"Aaah. Come on in..." as if he too had known me for a long time.

Beyond him I could see others of Them seated there. They had managed to assemble already. (The whole matter was despatched in half an hour, and I don't remember whether they even called themselves a commission.)

One of them, needless to say, was the Secretarial Type.

"Sit down," he said.

My memory may be playing me false. Maybe the police did the paperwork themselves and only then said they had better things to do than waste time on people fighting in lines and other such nonsense. They may have said it would most likely just be a fine, but... we would have to have a talk (and promptly sent us off to a different building with a room with an oaken Table, and a lot of civilians seated at it).

So it was in a different street and a different building that I saw the sturdy Table, and immediately noticed the familiar Proletarian Firebrand. He seemed also to recognize me, and said,

"Aaah. Come on in..."

And I went on in, and saw the rest of Them. And They were all exactly the same people.

Chapter 2

The Wise Old Man's seat is at the far end of the Table, to my right. He has a massive head and grey hair. He is a significant player and, of course, kindly, which is why the positive emotions (and in part the hopes) in my projections centre primarily on him. The Wise Old Man knows everything. He goes straight to the root of the problem, is not interested in settling old scores, and does not get bogged down in trivial detail. He will put his questions without splitting hairs or prying into motivations. He has no desire to turn the screw or unbalance you in order to score points off your confusion. He wants to get at the truth. He is a Wise Old Man.

All the time you are being quizzed and pushed and pulled about, and given no time to explain things properly, you remember (you never for a moment forget) that the Wise Old Man is in there, seeing the way they rush to judgement, seeing the way they won't let you get a word out, seeing how they get off on irresponsibly distorting your guilt. (You are guilty, but not in the pathetic way they are suggesting!) He sits there seeing and knowing: he is Wise. From time to time you look over in his direction to comfort yourself with the thought that he is there, albeit unspeaking. (The Wise Old Man's silence does get to you. It hurts and upsets you, but still you hope.) The person sitting next to him is the Grey-haired Woman in Spectacles. She is a woman in late middle age with a hint of the Caucasus in her face, and I am also pinning certain hopes of moral and explicit support on her. (I have been around. I know what makes people tick.)

Moving further in towards the centre of the Table, my expectations fall markedly. That is where the Pretty Woman usually sits, already cross at having to waste her time poking around in somebody else's private life (her golden time: time that is running out). She is flighty, and none of my hopes rest on her. In a bit further, and there is certainly also nothing to be said for the two relatively young men seated there. There is no point in even hoping: they are Wolves.

I had gone back that day to my former work place (having left in difficult circumstances). Already as I made the initial phone call I could sense their arousal (from the way they answered): now it was their decision that would count. I was in their hands. On the day appointed I saw that long oaken Table again, and there They all were seated at it, people I knew from my old job and people I didn't (but who were only too familiar). I looked with curiosity at faces ten years down the line from when I had last seen them, at the wrinkles and bald spots (if one can look with curiosity at a bald spot). I saw the weight they had put on, the grey hairs, until I came to someone I didn't know who was young and who even half rose from his chair, rubbing his hands in anticipation. "Well, shall we begin our little kangaroo court?" he asked smiling and revealing a set of teeth worthy of a crocodile. (A grand fellow, of course, totally dependable, one of us.) It was the first time I had heard one of these tribunals referred to with such casual familiarity, and just at the moment when I glimpsed those white, young faultless teeth. A Wolf, I thought, almost admiringly.

There was another young man of the same type sitting next to him. (There are always two.) Immediately after them, at centre Table, sat the obligatory Secretarial Type. The commission consists primarily of a Table with ten or twelve individuals seated at it, all on the same side (with one at each end covering their flanks). The other side of the Table is completely free: it is yours. There is a solitary chair in the middle of this empty side which is where you sit. The result is that their questions, or occasionally their abuse, come flying at you from an extended front, while you sit there turning your head to left or right.

It was a Young Wolf who had brought me down at an earlier tribunal by raising the topic of my mentally ill brother. In the even flow of any life (including mine) there are bound to be what a social security official might call "irregularities", or what I prefer to call hiccups. It is these hiccups (or irregularities) which as a rule attract the keenest interest at an interrogation. Once someone who knows what he is doing gets his hooks into such an irregularity (or hiccup), he can drag your entire soul out little by little after it, reeling it in like a fish out of deep water. (They will reel it in unhurriedly using quite a small hook but a sturdy line. They will haul your soul in while you try desperately to get it off the hook so it can slip back into the impenetrable depths which are its home.) The Wolf immediately moved in on my ill brother:

"I see you went on a foreign trip two years ago but told the Soviet authorities nothing about your brother."

I replied that the relevant questionnaire had not asked for that information.

"But it did have a question, 'Where do the members of your family work?' You concealed the true situation with some ingenuity. You wrote some vague nonsense about a factory..."

"He did work at a factory."

"You knew perfectly well that he was only attached to the factory, and temporarily at that. He is unemployable. Why did you conceal that fact?"

I had no answer. Of course I should have written the truth on that form (but my brother really did have a job at first). I should have been able to explain it all to them perfectly acceptably, but there had been some further considerations at the time which I could no longer remember: I had no answer. There was an awkward pause, and they immediately hooked me and starting reeling me in.

"What illness does he suffer from?"

"Um." Again I had no answer. (It was becoming a habit.) "I'm not sure exactly."

"Don't you take an interest in your brother's life? He really is your own brother?"

"Yes."

"Well don't you go to see him, don't you visit him? Surely it matters to you how he is getting on?"

Another pause. (How can you answer when they run one thing into another?)

"Do you really not know how his illness has been diagnosed?"

Pause.

I wanted to reply that of course I knew, but only approximately. I am not a doctor and the incomprehensible terminology for describing an anomalous schizophrenic illness is beyond me, but it was too late. The colour rushed to my face. I sat there mumbling wretchedly. *He does not even know what illness his own brother is suffering from.* The insinuation hung in the air. They had me hooked, and would now reel in my desperately resisting soul.

"How do you get on with your parents? Are they very old? Are they still alive?"

They were getting really personal, but I carried on answering, by now totally confounded.

"When did you last go to see them?"

I told them.

"More precisely. Can't you remember the date you went to see your own mother?"

From far over on the right-hand section of the Table the Ordinary-looking Woman asked, with a barely audible catch in her voice:

"How old is your mother?"

I was so thrown that I couldn't answer even that question. I told her of course what year my mother was born in, but then for some reason started counting up the years aloud.

In such cases, if you decide to answer them at all, you should say simply and succinctly that she was born in such-and-such a year, and leave it at that. (What's my mother's age to them anyway? What possible use can they have for the information?) Alas it is only later that your mind tidily arranges everything in its right place. Actually, of course, it does it in advance too (frequently at night). These are our night rehearsals when we think night answers through to the last nuance, arranging and structuring dialogue quite differently ahead of the following day's hearing. (My brother is just an irregularity for them, and you pitch all your psychic energy into erecting defences in advance and walling off the complexities of your life.) "A form of schizophrenia" is all the answer they need, and all the answer they should get (and you can all go screw yourselves...). Not a word more. And you should say it abruptly, with a look of contemptuous total openness on your face to put even the most practised of them off the notion of prying further into when and how exactly your brother became ill. A contemptuously laconic first answer can rule out all their subsequent would-be probings. "My mother is old, and no concern of yours."

Night thoughts are not only prudent (anticipating the questions of the morrow), but also far-sighted in the sense of sometimes penetrating the no-go area of their Freudian Id. Investigation of their Id begins with a night imagining of how my judges and interrogators would behave if the powers above suddenly allowed them free rein in the literal gratification of their desires. ("Tear off the veils, everything is permitted. Do whatever you feel like, right now. Nobody will ever find out.")

The Proletarian Firebrand is the least interesting in this respect. He would just want consumer goods (something tangible he could take off me if I couldn't defend myself). He is not greedy, and would be perfectly satisfied with a pay-off of some smoked fish or a dried bream. If he were freed of all propriety, he would probably rush round straightaway to my home and run from the spare room to the kitchen and back. (Like many other people in these hard times when you can't depend on the local shop and need to be able to hoard food, I have two fridges.) He would run around, slamming the fridge doors and rummaging among the jars inside them looking for the bream. The only additional (im)moral satisfaction he would need would come from my having had the weakness to offer him fish and friendship.

The Wise Old Man is a different matter. Even in my shrewdest night thoughts I have trouble picturing what he wants. He thrives on tragedy. He needs for me to realize that life is hard (a constant refrain of old age). He needs for me not merely to be tugged this way and that by questions and humiliated, but for them to whip and torture me too, and break me on a primitive rack in some Cellar, and after that he might perhaps find me innocent and feel compassion for me. (I am not exaggerating. We are talking here about the hidden mainspring of his psychology, an innermost secret desire which he himself, most likely, is not aware of. But the insights of night reveal everything, or almost everything.) He is too old and wise to be able to feel real pity until I have been whipped raw and had my bones broken in the Cellar, and my veins drawn out on the high rack. He would take me from the rack. He would take me from it himself and carry me in his arms, a strong, caring old man. He would carry me in his arms swaying slightly as he walked and singing a barely audible song like an old nursemaid. He would feel compassion for me.

Of course, the Table is related to the Cellar.

This is one of its physical attributes, like the strength of its oaken legs or its great length. (It has to be long to be able to seat them all along one side.) The association between the Table and the Cellar is substantive, unchanging, and goes back far into the depths of history, to Byzantine times, let us say. (And Roman times too, of course. I have no illusions about the Latin West.) No matter how civilized or artistic the way in which the bottles of Narzan mineral water are set out or casually disposed over its surface, the Table has always relied on the Cellar and been upheld by it, and this is one of its attributes and at the same time one of its mysteries. We should regard it as a mere fluke when the link is suddenly exposed, as in the sixteenth century under Ivan the Terrible's militia, the *oprichniks*, or in Stalin's cellars in 1937, in what I would describe as an unduly blatant manner.

This is why, as you walk out after even the most straightforward, insignificant discussion of your affairs, your spirits instinctively rise and you are walking on air. Yet at the same time you can feel in your water that you have not left them behind you for good, only slipped through this time, and that there will assuredly be a next time. Some Baize-covered Table to End All Baize-covered Tables still awaits you. (As yet it is only being readied.) You may well get away again next time too, but don't get too cocky about having got off scot free.

Old Volodya had been in the labour camps many times. When he was drunk he would upbraid every passer-by (it was never clear in what connection):

"Feeling pleased with yourself? Just you wait. You'll be pissing your pants soon enough!"

There was a certainty in his voice that some future tribunal inexorably awaited us all, but the ex-political prisoner soon gave up his prophecy and would then sit on a bench in the courtyard, hanging his head and talking quietly about his numerous women (who had all forgotten him, already!). You would hear fitful laughter and his muttering,

"Ha-ha-ha-ha... what tits... Louise... cancer... Vietnam rug..."

A Cellar you have been brought to swims up so offhandedly (unfrighteningly) out of the past. You have been delivered by one means or another to a chamber with dank vaults (or perhaps not dank, perhaps warm vaults) where you are to be beaten. The Cellar is a large, wide room but with a low ceiling, a huge low room, and your arrival rather catches today's executioners on the hop. One of them gets up and throws a surly look at the entering guards and you, the prisoner brought for beating. He has a mug of tea in his hands, a metallic mug from earlier years, and he is gnawing a chunk of sugar, not the friable parallelepiped of today's lump sugar, but a chunk of sugarloaf, again from those earlier years. Now he is drinking his tea holding the sugar in his teeth. It is his job to lash the victim half to death with a leather knout. He is well built, with intelligent eyes and an attractively sculpted high forehead. He drinks his tea, holding the mug and looking at you. A second torturer is standing next to him, a squat man with a vacant, mentally retarded look. His job is to punch the victim with his massive iron fist. He is vicious, and does not punch only when strictly necessary or when instructed to do so. (The two of them remind you quite spontaneously of that other pair who sit, or used to sit, or some day will sit, side by side at the oaken Table: the One Who Asks the Questions, and the dim-witted Proletarian Firebrand. They are the same people.) The Cellar is just the Table in a more tawdry and humdrum manifestation... But now a third man is coming towards you from the recesses of the Cellar. Who is he? A drowsy young executioner takes a few steps towards you (and those who dragged you here) from the depths of the Cellar. He has just got out of bed. They have beds here. They sleep here in their own part of the room. There are kettles, tea. It looks like a scruffy, down-at-heel dormitory, and only the front right-hand section of the Cellar, presumably the bit where the punching and whipping goes on and there is a lot of blood and snot, is paved with flagstones, since it is easier to swab paving slabs clean than conventional flooring. A Handsome Young Man has got out of bed and is coming towards you with a focused and unmistakably wolfish curiosity, and laughing moronically to himself ("Hih-hih-hih-hih!"), anticipating the pleasure he will have from this victim. He is naked to the waist and a heavy tattooed rose droops ornately on his shoulder. On his biceps there is another tattoo: a graveyard cross on a hill with a caption (which it is impossible to read as a mountain of muscle is constantly on the move, displacing the lines or running them together). A fourth man is still sitting on his bed mending something, a shirt apparently. His neatness and the needle in his hands make you think that this torturer would probably turn himself into a woman at the oaken Table, perhaps with a hint of prettiness, and like any other Pretty Woman would be cross at the pointless waste of time, and wonder, "For heaven's sake, how much longer are they going to go on interrogating this character?"

You cannot see any others for the moment. They are in the depths of the chamber. (You can only see the part of the Cellar immediately beside the entrance they brought you in.)

The Cellar as the Continuation of the Table by Other Means; and the Table as the Apotheosis of the Cellar. The daytime intellect sees their duality not so much in terms of time (past and present) as of two images which complement each other for all eternity: the Table with its red baize and sparkling decanter is Don Quixote with his dignity and the comeliness of old age; the Cellar is correspondingly Sancho Panza, unabashed by his workaday appearance, and scratching his belly which, in all likelihood, is tattooed and dirty.

Are the people seated at the Table aware of their invisible link with the Cellar? It is almost a rhetorical question, and while it is difficult to answer "yes", it is difficult too to give a definite "no". Neither does it matter all that much. The Table remembers for those seated at it. *The Table remembers.* That is the discovery I make this night as I pace up and down the corridor, slowly calming down.

The old Table stands there in the middle of the night, mindful of everything (even now it is standing there, somewhere). Remembering, it wants in the still of the night to join with the Cellar (just out of curiosity, just to see how things are going there). It begins to move out through the creaking door. End first, the Table eases itself past the door jamb, finally pushing through into the night-time Cellar and becoming part of it. It wants to coincide for a moment, to be the same place. Thus one image makes its way into the other.

The Wise Old Man. (He, after all, remembers too.) I am satisfied I have got him very nearly right. For a long time his sagacity, intelligence, vast experience and the numerousness of his years hid him from me (like mist), but it seems to me that now I do know what a principled Russian Wise Old Man would or would not do if left to exercise his will freely. It is not wisdom at all that is the mainspring of the Wise Old Man, but a particular kind of deep-seated compassion. The Cellar exposed him, making the impulses of his ancient soul more tangible. He has no need of details or lengthy casuistry when someone is being questioned at the Table. He would hand me over to the torturers in the Cellar without ado. Why drag things out, why put it off? And when they had whipped and tortured me almost to death, that is when he would come and take me like a child in his arms and feel compassion, and share in my suffering. They would torture and humiliate me, and then he would take me in his arms and say, "You have endured much, my son, but all this had to be. I had no choice..."

He will pity me sincerely. He will see that the end is already near and will think solemn thoughts about how much grief there is in each life on this earth. Yes, he stayed silent. He stayed silent all the time I was being questioned at the Table and while I was being tortured in the Cellar. He saw everything, understood everything, and said nothing. "But now I can tell you that I loved you like a son, and delivered you like a son into the hands of those brutes. It had to be. It had to be..." Carrying your broken body in his arms, he will walk back and forth till daybreak, the wise, compassionate old man.

(He is walking back and forth, and I hear his footsteps, the shambling of his old, tired legs.) And I am walking myself, and night is around me, this long, long night.

My wife is asleep. My daughter is asleep. The whole house is sleeping...

The worst thing is if your breath is affected: with each inadequate inhalation less and less air reaches your lungs. You are suffocating. The sticky perspiration of fear appears on your face and brow. (It is your heart again...) Your mind is racing: what should you do? Which of the medicines you have already tried many times before should you take now? Or perhaps you should take none of them, but just lie down and close your eyes? I sit at the dressing table, the drawer pulled out, quickly searching through the familiar boxes, medicine bottles, and twists of paper: medicine, medicine, medicine... With shallow breaths I read out the names, whispering them with just my lips. I lay them aside, I pick up new ones, all with quick, nervous movements of my fingers. I have something to look for and am quietly distracting myself from my fear. I sort through them, reading the names. It's a job for a pharmacist, but like any work it steadies your nerves.

When they were getting ready to go to bed and going off to their rooms, my daughter noticed my ill-concealed agitation. I find it more difficult to hide things from her than from my wife because I still forget she has grown up. She said:

"Don't get yourself in a flurry." (That is, don't let your thoughts upset you for the whole night.)

"What? What are you talking about?" I said, pretending not to understand.

Then she said more brutally,

"Do you want to die in the night like Prokofievich?" (This about our neighbour.)

"Certainly not."

She went on,

"Think how pleased They would be tomorrow: They wouldn't even have to give you a grilling. The comrade would already have received his punishment."

I laughed. She has a sense of humour. But I thought to myself, "No. She is too young to understand them yet. It really isn't that they want to punish me. Giving me a grilling is what they want, calling me endlessly to account, today, tomorrow, for ever more. To go over certain matters. To pry into my soul, and each time remind, not me, not themselves, but the Table they are seated at, its sturdy wooden legs, to remind it of the ceaseless accountability of every human life. It is not in order to punish, but purely to avoid excessive abstractness that they need somebody's particular life (tomorrow, mine). The place of inquisition is a narrow place, and if you manage to pass through they have no wish to punish you further. Let him get on with his life. He has got the message and we can leave it at that. They do not want to see you punished, and even less do they wish to see you dead. They want your life, warm, alive, with all its irregularities and blunders and mistakes and, absolutely crucially, they want you to acknowledge your guilt.

My wife is sleeping. There was a time when we slept together in a bed which was much too narrow. Then we had a wider bed but still we slept together, and if one of us got up in the night or early in the morning, the other immediately sensed the absence. (That side suddenly started feeling cold. Something was missing.) Now we sleep apart and even in separate rooms, and my little couch is quite enough for me. I have all I need. You have to be prepared for this. You are as alone again at the end as you are at the beginning.

I can hear her breathing behind the door of the room in which she is sleeping. I walk past, trying not to make a noise...

I really do not want to admit to my wife how violently my nerves get worked up (the ridiculous state of *total fear*) the night before I am called in for one of these talks. I must have concealed (from myself and from her) the first time this fear welled up in me. I did not admit to it then, and now have to carry on trying to conceal my weakness every time. I carry on, cockily pretending to rule the roost. (What can I do about it now? Nothing. I just have to walk it off on my own like this through one more sleepless night.) Of course, it is perfectly possible that she knows and is simply sparing my feelings. All her life she herself has been far more afraid than I am of these peer-group investigations and tribunals. She has made no secret of the fact and has just got used to it. But this fear has proved to be the sum total of my life too (what I personally add up to).

No matter what they are quizzing you about, they always manage to come round to how you are getting on at work. (It's a touchstone, after which they always unerringly discover the way of ease along which you are deviating from the steep and rugged pathway. They are good at that.)

I explain: it is just how everything came together. That is the way things are now. They say, "But what about your own concern? What about your own human concern and conscientiousness? Why on earth did you not point out that the work of the section was coming unstuck..."

I flare up:

"Just leave my work out of this! That's enough! You don't know anything about it!"

They could put me in my place there and then by pointing out that one of them is a qualified engineer, another a research worker. (They could crush me under the sheer weight of their degrees and qualifications.) Instead they do something much cleverer. They crush me with a long silence. They just say nothing, and their deliberate silence makes a complete nonsense of my shrill outburst.

Then a rather stout, respectable-looking man

who, for simplicity's sake, I characterize to myself as the former Party Man, says,

"All the same, one question: why did you not sound the alarm about how badly the work was going earlier?"

"Who to?"

"Surely that's obvious? To any higher management colleague."

(*Nervously.*) "I don't generally find myself chatting to them."

"You do have a telephone."

"I can't go phoning up one of the bosses just like that."

"You keep making your bosses out to be thoroughly alarming, but to all intents and purposes they are workers just the same as you. Why do you need all this alarm and despondency?"

I flare up again,

"Well I just don't go phoning bosses up!"

"Be that as it may, you could have made an appointment, or failing that simply have arranged to bump into someone in the corridor and mention the way things stood. Making it clear you were simplifying the situation."

"When the work of an entire section has been going off the rails for a very long time, when the whole damned shooting match is going down the tubes, it's best not to be schematic."

"Going off the rails, you say? Going down the tubes?! So you were in fact fully aware of the scale of the problem?"

"But..."

"Don't prevaricate. I want a straight answer."

"But I meant..."

"I said, don't prevaricate. Were you aware of the scale of the problem or not? Yes or no?"

And, straight between the eyes: "Yes or no?"

The fact that I am going to say "yes" is probably already written all over my face. Even though I am still holding out it has already developed there like an image on photographic paper. In coordinated cross-questioning of this kind you invariably find one of them who (for present purposes at least) knows all the answers and whose highly germane interventions get you hopelessly cornered. It is not that you have nothing to throw back at them, but that they are hydra-headed, and where there is diversity there is breadth. You and they cover unequal amounts of ground. If they don't get you the first time they jump you, they simply re-play their collective attack again from a different direction, from a third direction, five times, if need be, ten. There is no maximum, but as soon as they have got you nailed, that's the end and down comes the curtain. No re-match. You may now only pathetically answer "yes" with ritual self-abasement.

"Yes," I say.

The former Party Man now becomes an awesome figure.

"He does not even deny it," he says (referring to me).

He turns to all of them:

"I simply cannot imagine how he got away with it when he was young. I mean when he was God's gift to the opposite sex, and every little scrubber was telling him that now he would have to marry her." (This is a joke.)

(*Laughter.*)

The Party Man has not necessarily ever been a member of the Communist Party. He sits at the head of the Table to the left, a large man, so that this position suits him well, giving him room to move about. He has his legs stretched out in front of him. If he gets tired he can put his elbows on the table without troubling his neighbours. He sometimes proclaims his sense of superiority by quietly whistling a tune. (I used to take this as indicating that he felt comparatively unconstrained.) It does not go with his image or appearance. He only does it sometimes. Not often at all, really.

In earlier times he might have shouted and threatened to send you to the regional committee of the Party ("You will answer for this to the Regional Committee!"). Or even to have the KGB intervene. Needless to say it was only threats, bluster. When he shouted he partly revealed himself to the world. If he was in full throat his ample, rather baggy jacket would fall open and his tie would end up slewed to one side. He knew this happened and rather liked it. (He would be in no hurry to straighten it again.) If you looked at his eyes during such an outburst, however, goggling and bulging incongruously in that self-assured face, you became aware that this well-fed man had problems of his own in the struggle for survival, beside which your own paled into insignificance. The light grey suit, the already unmistakable paunch, the murderous detail and monstrous tensions of life in the jungle of the Party apparatus... Having done shouting, he would resume his earlier well-fed, manicured and calm appearance. His ailing heart would again be tucked away beneath the rolls of fat, at peace, and he would subside.

Already in the Brezhnev period (the end of an era) his influence was beginning to wane. There were other people who, seated at the Table, could both question better and assess guilt more surely than he. He continued, however, to regard the others seated at the Table as chess pieces (to be deployed by him in the course of the hearing). "Hmm, hmm. Quite right," he would murmur to himself in mild self-delusion (although it was not now he but quite different strict people who were doing the interrogating and nailing to the wall). He seemed to be commending their conduct of the case, as if to say, "Not bad at all. Well done!" Nowadays, if there should be some sudden slackening of the pressure, he will still join in himself. For an instant something twisted and deeply hidden will again flicker in his face. He will intone,

"Friends!" He likes that mode of address. He doesn't get complicated about the actual meaning of the word, but simply trots it out fluently and straightforwardly, as if wondering why there should be this unexpected stalling of such a well maintained machine (the machinery of the Confidential Talk).

"Let us, friends, ask him openly. We are not judges, we want to help. We want," and here he slows down, giving you a withering glance as he now turns to you himself, "We want to know how you think. That may even be more important than how you act."

He pauses dramatically, before adding a bullying,

"So tell us!"

Amazingly, you succumb to this power magic. You are suddenly filled with confidence in this bluff individual with his authoritarian smile (and undoubtedly high opinion of his own worth). The words you say are just what he wants to hear, sincere, simple words in unambitious sequence. How has he conjured them up in you (charmed them out of you)? It is difficult to say, but he has. He has the knack. At just the right moment he has given a lead, a direction, and now again the questioning flows of its own accord.

He has a vocation. He officiates at the mysteries of the tribunal not on behalf of himself but in the name of People Everywhere. There is even a hint of lethargy as he listens to the rest of them (seated at the Table). If you were mentally to strip this man down to his true nature, allowing him this very moment to show himself in his true colours, then in all probability his only immediate desire would be to soar in a half-dream like a bird above the general conversation (occasionally putting the tribunal right from above). The main attraction for him in this flight of the bureaucrat would be to take life easy, to forget everything. His other urgent desire would be to get up from the Table, come round and kick you in the stomach and the balls, see you double up and writhe for ten minutes unable to get air into your lungs. That's the way we need to treat you, my friend, for a start. After that he might really break away and soar like a big bird breaking away from sparrows and, spreading his wings wide, hover high in the air above where the hearing was continuing down here on Earth.

A calm man in a light grey suit, a winner, he

listens, slightly narrowing his eyes, as they quiz you. (Listen to them all shouting at once, going for you, arguing, interrupting!) He is in no hurry. He is in no hurry because he values his own opinion and does not want to be unceremoniously shouted down as if he were just anyone. Already in the Brezhnev years people started interrupting him if he went on too long, and so now he does not rush to have his say. He speaks when for one reason or another everybody else has fallen silent. A rare moment, but his own. He has no time for those who would contradict. He has no wish to share the illusion of his total power with anyone.

He fears disrespect, even the slightest. That is his great weakness today. He would find it unbearable if he were to say what he has to say and not be heard. (In the general melee it might not even be noticed that he had said anything.)

Chapter 3

She is adequately summarized as the Pretty Woman, and she sits to the right of the Table beyond the two dynamic young men. To be ruthlessly exact, she is an Almost Pretty Woman, interesting looking, good deportment, and in a class of her own, in present company at least. My misdemeanours are of no interest to her and neither am I. This ritual tormenting of a fellow human being is no skin off her nose. It will be somebody else tomorrow and the day after, and she does not see that as anything for her to get worked up about. For some unknown reason the individual on the other side of the Table has been picked for those assembled to hone their wits and vent their prurience and spite on. Men only really wake up when they're knocking ten bells out of their fellow men.

She is flighty and right now, as she sits at the Table, very cross. Her son will just have come home from school. Heaven knows what sort of dinner her husband will have got himself. She is not enjoying being here. Men are boring slobs. Look at the way they are going at this slouch, although he is just as much of a turn-off as they are. Why don't they just boot him out and be done with it? Not entirely to the point, she bursts out, "How can you believe someone like that? How can you waste so much talk on him? You ought to listen to yourselves!" (It is not clear whether she is annoyed with them or me.) "Do you have a proposal, Natasha?" the Secretarial Type asks. "No!" she says curtly. She looks down, twisting the ring on her finger. Much she cares. Suit yourselves.

She immediately looks up again peevishly at the One Who Asks the Questions. (The dear comrade has got the bit between his teeth. No stopping him now, and look at the time.) One of the Young Wolves sitting next to her whispers in her ear, but she is having none of it. She has had enough things whispered in her ear to last a lifetime.

The One Who Asks the Questions is, of course, Asking a Question. He has not lost the thread.

"You said that people in a queue are not human beings."

"Me?" (I only said I hadn't hit anyone in the line.)

"You said that people standing in a food queue cease to be human beings. They become a mob, and if somebody got beaten up, it was nobody's fault..."

"I said that?" (He is trying to push me over the brink.)

"For goodness sake, for some reason we are all sitting here, carefully listening to what you have to say. We may not be recording it, but we do have ears..."

The Young Wolf nearer the centre of the Table says,

"This old geezer seems to think he is the only person who ever stands in line, as if the rest of us don't do it every day in life!"

The Pretty Woman, still peeved, says,

"This old geezer doesn't seem to think at all."

The Party Man says,

"Friends, a person cannot open up his heart unless he chooses to. It is not only we who need him to be honest with us, this is something he needs himself."

The Party Man knows what he is doing and is not going to put his foot in it with a word out of place. (His standing in the community has been dented in recent years and he cannot afford to give any more ground.) He starts building his bridge into your soul with words which have stood the test of time, and you are amazed how skilfully he spins his (their) web out of nothing. They first cocoon your mind, and your heart stirs uneasily with the first intimations of guilt. These are ordinary people, sometimes fairly basic, but how well they have learned the art of burdening you with guilt feelings. Perhaps the mechanisms by which these inquisitions induce the sense of guilt lie deep in the psyche of the person under investigation. Somehow, the more conclusively the judgement of heaven has been mocked and undermined in Russia, the more these earthly tribunals have sprung up and come into their own. They not only abrogate the judgement of heaven, they appropriate its unbounded competence to their own ends.

This is why their members have the right to haul a man over the coals for the whole way he has lived his life and demand restitution, even though they are human beings no different from himself. "Pull me up if I have done something wrong! Carpet me for this" (usually trifling) "oversight. But don't call me to account for my whole life!" a body wants to howl, leaping from the chair and raising his hands (oh, yes) towards heaven. Sometimes people really do that.

"Sit down!" someone young (one of the Wolves) will immediately shout, reminding them of their place.

"We can do without the hysterics, thank you!" somebody else will shout (the Ordinary-looking Woman, seemingly an elderly schoolmistress).

And the person does sit down, brought to his senses, because they are right. It was hysterical. He feels he *is* guilty. It *is* your whole life that makes you behave (or misbehave) in a particular way. It *is* your life they have to judge. At this moment they are placed far above everyday cares and the sordid ways of human beings. No doubt they have sins enough of their own, and are even human beings with sordid ways themselves, but for the moment this is beside the point as they sit in judgement, invested with power and authority, partaking of the nature of the Dread Tribunal (and endowed, whether you like it or not, with some of its attributes). This is why their ponderous unanimity is such a complex matter. The sense that this is an earthly travesty of the judgement of heaven becomes even more substantial with the arrival of the Wise Old Man, who seats himself at the head of the table (to your right) and sits there omniscient and sage but, unfortunately, unspeaking. Also to your right, sitting next to each other as if the place belonged to them, are the two athletic young men with the restless energy and quick-wittedness of young wolves. They are just waiting to bare their white teeth in a grin and shout at you intimidatingly,

"Sit down! Sit down again! What are you

jumping up like that for?!"

Or, depending on the situation,

"Stand up! What do you think you are doing sitting down like that?"

Even in the ghastliest, most provincial little local magistrate's court, with its smells and its unswept floor and its greasy food wrappers under the benches, you breathe more easily than here. You sit in the dock and get busted under article such-and-such, clause so-and-so. When you are under investigation at one of these hearings, however, there are neither articles nor clauses, and the only way to redeem transgression is by changing the whole way you live your life. That is the only possibility. I am a man of my times and there is no changing me now. Like most of us I carry the image of their inquisition inside me for all time, a presence dreadful yet majestic, capable of insinuating itself into every nook and cranny of your soul and earthly being. For all that, you don't wholly credit them with divine authority. You hold back at least one or two crumbs.

The Proletarian Firebrand explodes. He is a down-to-earth bloke and makes no pretence of civility.

"You think you're the only person in the world, don't you! Just you at the centre of the universe!"

A simple drudge, he weighs in at the outset with a perspective from outer space.

"... There's just you, nice and cosy in the middle of everything, and working people can flog their guts out all around you. Is that it? But you expect someone to give you your bread and butter, don't you? Answer me! I am asking you a simple question: do you expect to be given your bread and butter?"

"Yes," I answer, "I do."

And so does he, but since he is the accuser here, the expectation of bread and butter counts against me. If I were the accuser in hot pursuit, no doubt I could hold the receipt of bread and butter equally against him.

There is no mollifying him. He gesticulates angrily, and through his bad teeth, some of them missing or knocked out, fly glistening globules of spittle.

"If everybody started thinking like you, I've got my bread and butter, so sod the rest of them, where would that leave us, eh?"

He repeats his enquiry,

"Where would that leave us? Nothing to say about that, eh? Well, I'll tell you where that would leave us. Everything would come to a standstill, that is where it would leave us. There'd be no lights to turn on in people's apartments, there'd be no running water! Get that into your head! The trolleybuses would stop running! The trains would stop running!"

And you do get that into your head. He's right about the trains, they would stop running; and the lights would go out; and there would be no water in the taps. You have to admire him, a crude good old boy spouting clichés, yet still managing to get to you. The rightness of what he is saying pushes your whipped soul a whisker nearer to feeling guilty. He is right. All of them are right.

The Young Wolf always tries a little too hard:

"...that's your signature there. You put your name on that sheet of paper too. You do remember your name, don't you?"

The One Who Asks the Questions knows the ropes better, and is given to wry utterance:

"Not every step is deliberate: but that does not, of course, mean you did not have an end in view."

(They are turning up the pressure now.)

The Party Man:

"That friend you were so keen to support went over to the other side. He went over to the enemy, didn't he, and spat on you from a great height."

Mumble some vague answer (how else can you respond?), and the Party Man will follow up straightaway, a professional among amateurs:

"I didn't catch that. Say it again, say it again! But don't change what you said the way you usually do. I insist he should repeat that word for word."

(Now the pressure is really on, as they try to get you to incriminate yourself.)

To your left sit the Proletarian Firebrand, the One Who Asks the Questions, and finally the Party Man (at the far end of the Table), a whole trinity of aggravation. I look straight ahead, with the result that in my peripheral vision their faces seem bathed in a milky mist.

Give them half a chance and they'll start on about the Russian people. They know my weak spot. (It's very easy to find a Russian's Achilles heel.) Your guilt feelings are not only instantly conjured, they crash down, stupefying you, a great sense of guilt which is the legacy of centuries of history. You thrash around in search of an answer, and never think to ask, "Well, what about the

Russian people, anyway?"

"What was your brother in hospital for?" (This is pea-shooting stuff. Small arms fire.) "Why did you register your son for a residence permit twice, no, three times even?" "Why, a hundred years ago, did you kick a Moskvich car in while in a state of intoxication, denting the side, getting yourself summonsed (we have the court record), and somehow managing to wriggle out of it. Why?"

Then there is the Secretarial Type, the Taker of Minutes, always more or less calm and collected. His is usually the first voice you hear, when you are barely in the door: "Come in. Sit down..." You peer at him, assuming the first person to speak must be the most important (a trap nearly everyone falls into). As soon as you do come in you are expected to repeat your name aloud and make sure they get your initials right for the record. You yourself are not yet there, even though you have come in. You go to the middle of the Table as They, as often as not, focus unexcitedly on your shoes and the way you walk. (There are clues to be found in the way a body moves his feet.) "Come in. Sit down...", and when you have come up to the Table he repeats the second part, "Sit down." The decanter's place is beside him. The first two things you see are the Secretarial Type's face and the decanter, both in the middle of the Table, the decanter full of water, the face full of affability. The Secretarial Type never has untidy hair and is never a large person. He is lean, his hair always tidy. He is neatly dressed, with a voice not low but not high-pitched either. He speaks in a readily intelligible, ordinary sort of way.

He doesn't ask for much. He wants to get his

word in when the discussion has already peaked, with an honest purposefulness which compares favourably with the motivations of the others, and which also means that he is never hostile towards you. All he asks is to be allowed to make his point, so that nobody should imagine he is only there to sharpen pencils and top up the decanter. He has a ballpoint pen in his hand, a stack of white paper in front of him, and he minutes things and takes notes with great dexterity. And he always has a white shirt on under his jacket. White is his colour.

"Come in. Sit down..." The Secretarial Type had once heard those crisp intonations (commanding but affable) in a dream like a voice from on high. He stored a mental recording of it in his mind for all time. It became not something he had copied, but something he had created. Five or six years ago a colleague at work told him his jokes smelt like home-brew and fresh cow pats. Since then he has given up telling jokes, finding it too stressful. If Siberian relatives from Tiumen descend on him he gets drunk with them, makes a lot of noise and laughs a lot, but when they leave that's the end of his three-day outburst and it's back to reality.

One time one of these tribunals was building a case against our colleague N. (who was something of a legend). He was an awkward customer, always at other people's throats. Obviously he was "guilty", but something else came out in the wash. In trying to defend himself N. told them about the death of his wife two years earlier. He told them about the loneliness which had made him quarrelsome, per-haps imagining they would sympathize. They found out, however, that he had bullied her, and one or two people on the other side of the Table knew something about their less than happy domestic circumstances.

They found out the reason he did not get on with his wife was because he frequently indulged in "business trips", during which he consorted with the various women he met up with. There was no throwing his questioners off the scent. One of his women had actually been a very young girl who, as they used to say, he had ruined. In his agitation N. even told them the girl's name. At least he remembered it. He had ditched her, and the young woman had been so shattered that she suffered a minor but protracted mental illness. That got them going, and they started in relentlessly on a related line of questioning which revealed that these business trips were often far from necessary and were, of course, claimed as expenses from his enterprise. And so on and so forth. His manifest and apparently unrelieved guilt was pumped out of him, although in reality, as with any human being, it had occurred piecemeal over a whole long lifetime.

The judges, his own colleagues, by this time knew perfectly well that they were sticking their noses into matters which were none of their business and that they ought to have confined themselves to N.'s argumentativeness at work. They were, indeed, way out of order but, having excavated practically the whole of his life, they could not simply fill it in again like some trench and walk away. There they were, seeing all his sins, like God... They carried on questioning, and N's guilt carried on mounting up. He was horrified himself at the things he had got up to. In the end, there it was, emptied all over the old baize-covered oaken Table, the guilt of an entire lifetime. The Last Judgement. N. was a broken man. He was admitted to hospital and died shortly afterwards. Somehow a light just went out in him, although there were those who said he had *done away with himself* by taking an overdose of tranquillizers.

All of us who had worked with N., almost all of us, suddenly realized he had been a decent, honest man, kind, in fact loyal, even if that could not neutralize all the bits and bobs we had excavated so single-mindedly. Anyway, we felt we were no better.

The One Who Asks the Questions is an intellectual and, to all intents and purposes, the leader of the pack. He adopts a level tone of civility whose effectiveness is not to be underestimated. He draws a lot of personal stuff out of you, not necessarily things you are ashamed of.

"What's that? What did you say?" Two, perhaps three of them, shout in unison, suddenly alert. They have caught the scent of some word I have dropped carelessly, and immediately they are on to a new, fresh track in the snow.

I have not yet realized what exactly has slipped my tongue, some chance verbal effluent, some protruberance of my disgruntlement, but they are on to it.

"What's that? What did you say? No, no, don't try to hide it. Those are your own words. We have detected the *protruberances of your disgruntle-ment.*"

They carry on excavating their trench, digging hole after hole wherever they spot an unevenness on the surface of your soul, holes and pits, caves and caverns, and they peer into the darkness and gibber, "How dark it is in there!" They dig the caves themselves, and then are surprised there is no light in them.

You answer their questions, haltingly perhaps, but without getting yourself in too much of a fix but then, at some quite unexceptional moment, you suddenly stop talking and, as if in a trance, as if someone had shouted, "Stand up!" (although nobody has), you slowly get up from your chair and then, realizing that this moment is no different from any other, you slowly sit down again in complete silence. But the chair collapses under you, the floor caves in. You are in the Cellar and that massive figure is moving in on you. There are whips and straps on the walls, hideous knives and pincers, but more than these details what holds your attention is this great, sturdy man with a not unattractive face who is coming towards you, to admit you. He has that rose with a twining stem tattooed on his shoulder, and the graveyard cross on his biceps. He is massive, half naked, with a suggestive gleam in his grey eyes, a huge stud who, as he puts it, likes having a bit of fun. When he is roused it is all the same to him whose butt is in front of him, man, woman, or sheep, just as long as his victim bleats and shrieks with pain. (Not just from the humiliation – an emotion he doesn't understand – but from pain. He prefers them to squeal the place down. He understands that.)

Even if you knew nothing of the Era of the Cellars or the Era of the White Coats, you still know about them only too well. The metaphysical pressure from the collective mind on the other side of the Table draws its power from the fact that we have no option but to bare ourselves. The only surprise is that we do not strip ourselves completely naked.

We bare ourselves, we bare ourselves sincerely, but we nevertheless conceal *something*, some small, stunted, insignificant thing. A few blades of grass survive, even as the oak trees, bushes, and turf are pullęd up by the roots. Two or three blades of grass... For some reason we keep these tokens of rebellion from them.

Perhaps they are calling me in because they want to edge towards sacking me. (The work force is being scaled down.) They would never dream of just saying this is the situation and we need to reduce the work force. They will call me in, talk about me, dig around in what I am doing now or have done in the past. They need to compromise you before the "moment of truth" when they boot you up the backside. While I've been preparing myself in the middle of the night for hundreds of questions they might ask, I have missed the most important question: Why are they calling me in? But actually that question does not matter. It is meaningless. The point is that the same old Table will be there, with the same people sitting round it, digging up the same old life. Mine.

They are incapable of saying anything straight out. They are inherently devious. They will set about questioning me, and the ghost of the Party committee of earlier years will hover over the old Baize-covered Table, not disturbing them in the slightest. Not everybody is afraid of ghosts. The old Table recognizes familiar intonations. (They call you in not to inform you of a decision, but to "Have a Talk" with you.) Of course I am Soviet to the toes of my boots, but so are they. They don't have it in them just to kick me out. They have to convince me that I am a useless shit who has made a complete mess of his life and that for some time now I have been a burden and an abomination to society. No matter how long I spend preparing like this in the middle of the night, they are going to catch me out over something. Just as surely, I am going to flare up the moment it becomes evident, towards the middle of our little chat, what they are really driving at (no earlier than the middle: they have to really be out to get me). I shall start thrashing about, resisting, snapping at them, and they, upping the ante tenfold, will pursue and play a *guilty* quarry who is trying to break loose.

It is night. The kitchen. I am, of necessity, brewing up an old-fashioned remedy my grandfather would have recognized from a collection of herbal ingredients assembled during the summer: valerian root, peppermint, river trefoil. What choice do you have if there's nothing in the pharmacy nowadays, and my heart, if not reined in towards night, tends to start fluttering like a frightened butterfly taking flight? (I picture the human heart as a red butterfly sitting with its folded wings rising and falling rhythmically in half breaths.) I shake out two spoonfuls of the mixture and place an enamelled saucepan in a large bowl of boiling water. The fear of death has taught me the art of the bain-marie. The night is long.

My hair is dishevelled, I look ill. I shuffle a slow, small-hours-of-the-morning shuffle past the mirror. I would give my reflection a wink but cannot see my eyes under their sagging brows and lids. I am dog tired.

A medicinal smell is coming from the kitchen. Time to go back. I see from my watch that it is time to turn down the gas if the bowl is not to boil dry.

It may be that I already have a better understanding of what makes the people sitting round that Table tick than they have themselves, but the knowledge does not, alas, give me the strength to distance myself from them. They are too close. I experience, of course, belated puzzlement as to how it came about that, having been tied to them for so long, I can now no longer live without them, or imagine myself free of them.

I come back down the corridor. If my shuffling feet wake my wife I shall tell her I have just this minute got out of bed. To go to the toilet. I may even decide to tell her I can't sleep, but then I'll be stuck with her sympathy. I should be glad to accept it if I could also bring myself to tell her about the pathetic fears preying on me. Perhaps she already knows. She may realize it is easier for me to get by without sympathy. Every family has its secrets. In ours it is these hidden night fears of mine.

They have questioned me dozens, perhaps hundreds of times before and I have lived to tell the tale, so what difference is one more time going to make? The whole problem is, however, that it is not the 148th interrogation that crushes a person, but the accumulated legacy of the previous 147. That is for sure. How many times I have outwitted them as they sat behind their Table, throwing them off the track, fooling and tricking them, or simply proving more intelligent than they were and having more insight into the situation. Sometimes I chose concealment, sometimes behaved defiantly, sometimes compromised, sometimes steeled myself to take them on over small things or large. For their part they barely reacted, just remained who they were, not changing their expressions or trying anything on, and that meant they had won. One day I realized they were part of me, and that there was no getting away from their archetypal faces and questions. One night, a night just like this one, as I was preparing myself for a questioning, I did manage with enormous mental effort to see them for what they were, but at the same instant they saw me for what I was, and became part of me. We were one. Of course, there is no getting away from them now. There is no time left anyway. My life is over. I do regret thinking obsessively about them. I do regret that here I am on a sleepless night tensely boiling up dark violet valerian root and shuffling round a darkened flat instead of being asleep. I feel sorry for my ego which has been turned into plastic from communing with them at their Table and which, if held for a moment in front of their flame, softens and folds, its warmed side sagging into a latticework of wrinkles.

Every man is destined to face judgement one way or another. For each of us there is either an awe-inspiring Judgement in the style of Michelangelo, a time of reckoning for our sins at the end of life, or a couple of hundred little kangaroo courts along the way at a Baize-covered Table, staring fixedly at a decanter of water. Perhaps this is just the Russian way. Then I wonder whether those 147 or 148 confessions don't mean that I have already been through my purgatory. Perhaps someone who has been subjected to questioning from his schooldays onwards as to how and why he has been living his life, himself a particle of the Russian people but always guilty of failing them, perhaps he, poor bugger, at the end of his life will suddenly get a whopping discount, and be told, "No Last Judgement for you. Go on in! That's all right. Nothing to declare. You have already come clean on all our questions. Go on in. Forward, *homo sovieticus*, you have nothing more to worry about!" And you are not afraid to see the gloom and darkness ahead of you. This time it is only night.

(Given an existential choice my ego would have chosen to live life with a flourish, dishonestly even, from the viewpoint of conventional morality. I would like to have been a thief, a talented cat-burglar enamoured of urban apartments on the lower floors, their lights out for the night. Perhaps that is the life I would have chosen, if nothing spicier! But no. I wasn't up to it. It never was an option. They did not even leave that open to me, burdening me from childhood with that sense of guilt.)

What an odd scene I suddenly imagine (just what I don't need right now). I picture a punch-up at their Table. Yes, a real fist fight breaking out among Them. Three of them slogging it out against four, while two others are having it out between themselves on the sidelines. Swearing, shouting, impacting knuckles. A chair thrown at someone arcs over the oaken Table, albeit without desecrating the decanter or the bottles of Narzan.

It is a vivid fantasy. I have just arrived. You would think I would view the scene with satisfaction and take my leave, but I stand there at a loss. I have come to bare my soul. I am ready for their questions, ready to explain myself. I have brought them my life to work over, but they are otherwise engaged. What am I supposed to do, where am I supposed to go if they are all in the thick of a fight? I stand and wait, shifting from one foot to the other. I need their tribunal. They can't just leave me alone with my soul. It doesn't belong to me any more. Take it! Please, take it!

Chapter 4

If you attempt to generalize the people seated at the Table, you are subjected to a kind of disagreeable night hearing in your own mind. If you don't, chaotic fear clutches directly at your heart. (Night thoughts are disturbing, but if you do not pull them into some kind of order they are crippling.) Order your thoughts and you bring some kind of order to the way They will behave at the Table tomorrow. Tomorrow you should be all right, but not necessarily the next day. (One of these days your butterfly will just flap its wings and flutter away.) But there is something specific at the back of my mind: what?

I try to remember. Ah, I know. The Grey-haired Woman in Spectacles, the soft-hearted one at the right-hand corner of the Table who looks half Russian and half Armenian or Jewish, is evidently not going to be there tomorrow. I heard someone mention it. They were talking on the telephone as I was walking past. I'm one vote down. Although even she might speak against me. (It does happen.) Still, just knowing she was sitting there over to the right with those sad eyes behind the lenses of her spectacles was comforting. She would have been sitting there with her grey hair, wearing those thick spectacles of hers, reeking of cigarette smoke. (Too bad!)

The psychiatrists of the Era of the White Coats

did not believe for a minute that the person sitting in front of them was a saboteur or enemy, or a would-be assassin of the Party leadership. (Explosions, shootings, and "enemies" in general had been left behind in the peak purge year of 1937.) The offence of the dissidents was merely an unwillingness to "march at one with the Soviet people". Anybody who did not want to do that (now that there were no more Enemies of the People) must be mentally ill. That is what the White Coats were there to demonstrate. They had to label the culprit: "mentally ill". They were perfectly sincere in their belief.

The mental illness of dissidence could prove treatable by a course of therapy in a psychiatric clinic. It was not a matter of helping an individual called A.V. Ivanov. You were aiding the emergence of the potentially healthy Soviet human being within A.V. Ivanov. Expert medical hearings were conducted by a variety of people from a variety of backgrounds, who found themselves invited to the Table in a variety of ways but, as always, next to the Secretarial Type sat an intellectual with a high, handsome forehead, the Doctor Who Asks the Questions. The Wise Old Man was there too (a little old man representing lay interests). Then there was the Proletarian Firebrand (a low-ranking doctor who simply could not get his career together), and the Pretty Woman Doctor. In other words, a fair cross-section of society, only wearing white coats. (In a sense they *were* the Soviet People, which gave scope for the person seated in front of them to feel suitably guilty and open his heart to them.)

The Secretarial Type's ballpoint pen worked

overtime. The Era of the White Coats was his era, the only period when his records mattered and the words of those conducting the hearing really had to be taken down with scrupulous exactitude. Sometimes (to defeat a springtime draught) the Secretarial Type would pin his white sheets of paper to the Table with hypodermic needles when these were finally no longer reusable (thumbtacks were unobtainable), and the old Table under its cloth then bore a succession of fourfold stigmata. It is years, of course, since they have caused it pain, but the black dots are still there, though veiled by the dust of time. The old Table also bears (beneath its cloth) the elongated black scars of cigarette burns. The tablecloth, of course, is regularly changed (the cloth has been replaced many times), but the Table has a physical memory of these scars burned into its old body. Through the slumber of decades it remembers the voices too.

The voices of those who usually sat before it were not loud, although they were counted not singly but in thousands, even tens of thousands, and came from many different towns. Young people, mainly. Time had thrown up a whole generation which, if only by a hair's breadth, did at least differ from its predecessors (a possibility conceded by biology). Perhaps, though, they did not even differ by a hair's breadth, but were merely of an age when doubt and confusion of spirit are the norm; and when they had passed through this period in a year (or a year and a half) every one of them would have turned into a perfectly conventional Soviet citizen, upright, and even believing (in his own way) in certain ideals,... but they were not given that year (or year and a half). If a young person stuck his neck out, came to official notice, and was detected saying something ill-considered, he was dragged resisting before the Baize-covered Table.

Strictly speaking, in the first instance it was not the White Coats at all who were called to judge these young people. In the first instance there was a hearing before a works or student representative committee (a Table with people seated at it); then an appearance before a community court (already a Baize-covered Table with a Decanter); and finally, a board of doctors and psychiatrists with lay representation (the third and final Table). In effect they were all the same Table, only extended threefold on this occasion.

And here is what awaited these young people: the destruction of their mind by medical means; followed by "docility"; followed, as a rule, by an early and unremarked death.

On the same section of the Table as the Pretty Woman Doctor sat the Ordinary-looking Woman (who seemed likely to be a schoolmistress). If you touched the old Table just where she was sitting, your hand when you took it away would surely be redolent (through the new baize) of school desks and thin school exercise books. By this time schools had already done away with inkwells: the new ballpoint pens were everywhere much in evidence. In psychiatric clinics, however, a drug was still in use which was popularly known by the pretty name of Alionka (after the heroine of a famous Vasnetsov painting). Sometimes it was called Ezhevika (Bramble), because of its dense, dark red colour. This was a patented compound of insulin and two old-fashioned preparations (barbital and urethane). Alionka was much in vogue in psychiatric hospitals. It was assimilated almost immediately and, most importantly, equally rapidly induced a lasting state of drowsiness in the patient, depression and, admittedly, sometimes also permanent loss of intellect. (It also induced a bizarre phobia of birds. All the patients talked about birds.)

The young men and women (university students or lecturers), summoned one after the other to face the assembled experts, responded pertly. They were impudent, sharp-tongued, and thought it all a bit of a lark. They even, within bounds, laughed at their medical judges. "Do we really look like nutters? If we are nuts, who isn't?" His distinguishing feature was a shock of blond hair. She, called in after him (they stuck together right through until the therapy), had striking, regular features and a small beauty spot on her cheek. Neither had long to live.

She was slender. The cocktail of subcortical toxins administered during treatment very soon reduced her to docility. The laughter disappeared and her expression became thoughtful. A silence enfolded her, although she heard the raindrops falling on the roof, or the ticking of a clock. Later on, as happened with all of them, she was subject to outbursts of rage at the sight of pigeons scrambling for breadcrumbs. She experienced an unbearable revulsion for birds of any description, but especially large birds, crows or pigeons. She would stamp her feet at them and shout "Shoo, shoo!", and as soon as the startled birds flew up off the ground she would be overcome by period pains and nausea, and break out in a heavy sweat. She soon died. She was spared the succession of fits usual in such cases, but became emaciated and died unobtrusively. He took longer to die. He had a powerful intellect which held out for one month, even two. He even continued solving theoretical problems of some description and proving theorems. He slept, ate, and even joked. Yes, he carried on joking, as he had when first brought before the Table for judgement. He carried on for quite some time, even after they had mentally disabled him, even after his mind had gone flat like a car battery. The jokes kept coming, leaping from his lips. He showed no inclination to fall silent right up until the moment of death. (The only standard symptom exhibited was the phobia of avians.)

The medical and psychiatric judges were themselves not by any means immune to side-effects from these inquisitions. In exposing a fellow human being's soul, they came up against natural reactions which (for them) constituted a pernicious psychological influence. The doctors were to admit that questioning someone who had been delivered into their hands (at their Table of judgement) entirely without redress, had a marked effect on their own psychology. Sometimes they became depressed, but sometimes it produced a playful arousal which they did not care to analyse. For a doctor who was not himself a hundred per cent stable, participating in these interrogations could prove psychologically unbalancing and push him to the virtually unsignposted borders of the pathological. Intercourse resents half-measures. In interrogation one person is using another. Penetrating someone else's heart and mind to search for something is closely akin to rape.

One of the doctors, the One Who Asked the Questions, was a genuine scholar who had spent his entire working life thinking about dry plasma, insulin, and presentation of psychotropic drugs in ampoules. He felt sorry for Her on a purely human level, and was genuinely saddened when her mind suddenly lapsed into a twilight state. He liked her, and when after long resistance and unwillingness to explain various student mischiefs her heart was finally melted and she said, "I will tell you. I will tell you everything...", only stumbling for a moment on the threshold of total confession, the doctor gave a sigh of relief (and unexpectedly, as he subsequently admitted, felt sexually attracted to her).

Her beautiful young body was placed temporarily in an ancillary cold room awaiting transfer to the mortuary the following day and, as noted in a subsequent deposition, he "remained alone with her unable to tear his eyes from her face and the birthmark on her cheek". After the depression, the snuffing out of her intellect, and the attacks of phobia of pigeons and sparrows with their detestable cooing and twittering, the patient had died. She had died and now lay here, alone, in a chilled room. Her doctor, however, stood just inside the doorway contemplating her sadly, and as yet not aware (be it noted for the record) of deriving pleasure from the situation until "later that night he found himself alone with the young woman's body. His desire proved so great, and the circumstances so propitious, that he was unable to resist exposing his penis and touching it to the thigh of the corpse, experiencing great sexual arousal. Completely losing control of himself, he embraced the body and applied his lips to the private parts. According to the accused" (now it was his turn before the tribunal) "he became so sexually excited at that moment he ejaculated. He was immediately overcome with pangs of remorse and fear of discovery by the night nurses or cleaners. Towards morning he returned again, immediately sucking at her breasts before applying his lips to the private parts." Presumably rigor mortis and the chilled state of her body frustrated full sexual intercourse (thereby frustrating also the bringing of a much more serious charge under the relevant article of the Criminal Code). Various admissions scattered through the record of the interrogation indicate beyond doubt that it was precisely his participation in the process of extra-judicial questioning which stimulated him. As a psychiatrist he had earlier experienced emotional reactions towards women he was questioning (he would feel out of sorts, or frustrated, but insisted that he was never previously aware of the sexual nature of his frustration). Further investigation and meticulous checking of records of his times on night duty bore out what he had to say about earlier cases, and also the gradualness of the build-up of his feelings. Was he similarly aroused when subjecting men to intensive questioning? Apparently not. He was perturbed only while interrogating women, and recognized the nature of his emotions only after condemning that young woman to therapy and seeing her die shortly afterwards from the administration of Alionka.

I suspect that ritual sex has not infrequently been associated with interrogation and judgement. The link must surely go back to the earliest times and the customs of ancient tribes. I find this thought profoundly disturbing. Two paces from the inquisitorial Table yawns an abyss.

Chapter 5

Interrogating someone is tantamount to stripping them naked and copulating with them. Every successive item peeled off excites and inflames those seated at the Table, and also us, the interrogated (in our passive role). But then there is no consummation. They have stripped you bare with their questioning; they have passed you round from one to the other; they have gang-banged your soul, but this has been the safest of safe sex, with no transfer of body fluids. The incompletion of the act is obvious, and the symbolic decanter (of which nobody ever avails himself) stands as pointlessly in the middle of the Table as a standing stone, a ritual phallus. The moment their victim escapes through the door, a sense of *coitus interruptus* overwhelms the judges. He has escaped. He has got away. Their little inquisition immediately wilts. They even look round at each other as if wondering, "What are we all still sitting here for? How pointless!"

Geosexology. This word's time has come. The general outline of my concept is: in Latin America, sex and blood; in America, sex and dollars; in Russia, sex and tribunals; in Europe, sex and..., um... Oh, yes, obviously: in Europe, sex and family. Fancy forgetting. (But it is night. My sense of humour is failing. Humour needs a rest sometimes too.)

The upshot is that, whether they know it or not, having subjected your soul to their unbridled collective voyeurism, your interrogators are now in urgent need of literal, physical release in good old biological sex. However they may explain it to themselves, the fact of the matter is that they are in a tearing hurry to get their rocks off. Any grey little act of gratification will do as long as it is soon. (They also have the perfect opportunity: a few more hours' absence which don't have to be justified to a wife or husband.)

There could, however, be a much loftier explanation: their duty now is to conceive a new soul, to fructify chaos (they consider themselves no worse than God). Having usurped the role of the Creator, they find themselves saddled with His interminable problems. Having brought one life to a culmination with their Judgement, it is incumbent upon them now to conceive a next one. Since creating new life out of chaos or clay is still, for the time being, a bit beyond them, the moment their little day of judgement is over each of them runs hell for leather to the nearest bed for a good screw, the women no less than the men, in deference to a tiny gene which maintains the relationship between death and life. (They have no choice in the matter. They have to perform in accordance with their ontological programming, automatically creating a new life as they close down an old one.)

Immediately to the right of the Secretarial Type, squeaky clean Taker of Minutes, sit the two Young Wolves. One of these is the Wolf Who Is Not Dangerous. (Not here, at least. In other contexts he rips off anything he needs: a position at work, a woman, a floozy, fast bucks, booze. He is always in a hurry, and always ravening.) Here, however, he is bored. He doesn't give a damn for any of them. In general, of course, he goes along with the questioning, but just sometimes, precisely because he doesn't give a toss, and because there is an intrepid side to him, he is quite capable of suddenly lending his support to you (the victim sitting out front in the middle of the Table). He is quite capable of arguing in your favour, or suddenly snapping and snarling at the One Who Asks the Questions or the Party Man, as if to say, "Don't tell me what to do. I know the score as well as you."

He is, however, intrigued by the experience of the tribunal. He would not want to miss the detail of how they trap you. He has been bored up till now, but his eyes lazily open, checking that he hasn't dozed through that exciting moment when they are finishing you off and you are just about to break. (A vicarious predatory thrill. This is the moment. He is mentally picturing how he will get his own immediate superior on his back on the floor and savage him the moment the old watchdog starts slowing down. He'll hear him squeal yet...!)

"Why are you trying to crawl away?" he suddenly shouts indignantly if the victim (you, groggy from the questioning) is as good as dead, broken-backed, but still with enough strength left to spin it out a bit longer, to carry on justifying his actions and trying to crawl away from his just desserts (and still showing no sign of shedding the tears they really need, sincere, bloody tears of contrition).

He is on the way up, collecting bonus points at work, already enjoying a bit of respect; he is climbing the ladder, growing and (when no one is watching) already basking in his own self-regard. He is still a Young Wolf at heart but no longer mauls and savages everything on sight.

He enjoys the situation where someone is petitioning him, standing alongside him and looking earnestly into his eyes while talking to him. When he comes in to the Table of inquisition he will seat himself down close to the decanter of water; not because he is thirsty, of course, but because he already senses, and is accustomed to the idea, that his place is close to the centre of power. He has not made it yet, however. He strides along with some pathetic character bobbing beside him, probably a friend of whoever they are about to give a good grilling to (a buddy of the victim for today). He bobs along, trying to find the right moment to put in a good word. This, needless to say, is a moment for firmness:

"No. No, I'm making no promises..."

The other persists with his absurd grovelling:

"Heaven forbid, I wouldn't dream of asking you to promise anything. I know how even-handed you are. I just wanted to mention... I just thought... I think possibly..."

"No. No promises."

For all that, however, this ambitious young Wolf Who Is Not Dangerous does not abruptly walk off in the opposite direction. Indeed, he does not even turn his head away. He allows his petitioner, or semi-petitioner, to carry on walking alongside. He even allows another semi-petitioner, who tags on from the right, to say what he has to say and walk beside him (although he gets no promises either). He would be perfectly content to have the one on the left, and the one who has just come running in from the right, carry on walking along beside him just as they are, and looking into his eyes while they are talking, and asking him some favour for the whole of (what he hopes will be) his long life.

"No. No promises."

He sees an admirable reflection of himself and you and me flitting around him as he walks, in the eyes of other people. He has turned from the lifts and is proceeding down the corridor. He walks steadily, while we rush along trying to keep up with him. We rush along trying to tell him something which (we believe) is important.

The other Young Wolf is more extroverted. He is bursting with energy and wit. (The wellsprings of vitality bubble from the very depths of his nature bringing up an amazing, vivid smile to his face. You can positively feel the life force in him.) His type is well liked or, to be more accurate, popular. People like the smile: it does you good just to look at it. It has to be said, however, that he will be the first at the hearing to address you over-familiarly, to punch below the belt, or suddenly yell, "What way is that to sit? What are you slouching for?" He will bawl you out without worrying too much about the finer points of the situation, and drive you into a corner with direct, and if you allow him to get away with it, shaming questions.

The Young Wolf Who Is Dangerous is danger-ous for wanting to maul anything any time any place (but in particular here, at the Table of inquisition). Turning a situation to his own advantage is something he does without a moment's reflection because mauling is now a reflex, as basic to his nature as an instinct. (You are the pay-off; everything you have is the pay-off; your whole life is his pay-off.) If you are at bay and lose your footing, it makes sense to rip something off you. How about your old woman, assuming she is not too old. If she is fat and good-natured, so much the better! He might have a go at your daughter too. Eighteen years old or thereabouts: not someone to kick out of bed. Except that eighteen-year-olds can be more trouble than they are worth. You ditch them and then start feeling sorry for them. Forget it. Make it easy on yourself. Stick to the wife!

So when your wife turns up a day or two before the tribunal and wants to have a word with somebody influential (she asks anxiously what the procedure is; she is shaking slightly), the young Wolf is at hand to oblige. He isn't even aware of being deceitful, because now he is in his element. "Yes, madam, I should be able to help. Yes, that is within our competence. We shall do our best to sort everything out for you. When I see someone sincerely troubled, my heart goes out to them." His eyes dart forward trying to establish eye contact. No, no. He is not after money. (He is, but for the moment he is after something more exciting.) No, no. Who said anything about money? You are a woman: work it out for yourself. Then after a moment he dives straight in. There is no holding him. He is a Wolf:

"How about me coming round for tea? I think

during the day would be best, when it is nice and quiet."

And, with a smile,

"We could have a little drink together, just you and me. How about it?"

Of course, in your time you have sat on the other side of the Table yourself, among the judges. (Everybody has. Everybody has been part of the line-up.) Our consciousness is half controllable and if, when you were seated at the Table of judgement and it was your turn to speak, you felt some psychological block, you faltered for only a moment before, apparently willingly, speaking out, lapsing into that helpful (if alien) interrogator's jargon.

As you moved from youth into more mature years, it was inevitable that you would be one of that pair of Young Wolves. It was pretty dull stuff, but against that you enjoyed the favour of the woman sitting next to you. (At first she sat some way off, but you moved closer to her after one or two hearings.) She could certainly be accounted Pretty, and your youthful wolfish leanings were additionally stirred by her evident maturity and correspondingly greater emotional experience; also by the fact that she had a husband. Admittedly shortly afterwards you ceased to be bidden to the inquisitorial feast, but this was a matter of chance, and after life had given the box a good shake and made you more vulnerable (and increasingly sympathetic towards those who found themselves being questioned).

The bald bigamist... How adroitly he manoeuvred, finding excuses for himself. How far ahead he would suddenly start directing that sincere voice of his towards evoking human fellow feeling, the sympathy he so wanted from us; until I asked, "Are you going to tell us about *all* your women?" He smiled ruefully and replied, "I shall have no choice." But I went on, "Not *all* of them, *please.*" After that unspectacular and rather relaxed bullseye all the fight suddenly went out of him. He deflated (instantly, in front of our eyes, and yet how jaunty he had been!). Having landed a punch on my fellow man, I immediately felt the thrill of the chase, the savour of persecution. A gap opened up in his self-justification (rendering him vulnerable) on another flank, and I jabbed right in there: "Would you agree that you talk rather a lot about Andrei Ivanovich and his wife? Why should that be, I wonder...?" At that he lost heart completely, his voice went hoarse, and his spleen gurgled in anguish (not a sound I had heard before). Andrei Ivanovich was a big boss. It was a clear foul to hit him with a boss. I had not intended to show the situation up so obviously, not at all. I was simply following a trail, wearing him down, chasing, harrying, and the boss, our fat authority figure, was a rod to beat him with. In the excitement of the hunt I rodded him.

Checking and putting someone else's life on the right tracks, moulding it, creating it, no less: creating everybody else's lives and putting right everything that was wrong. Great! The upright Soviet citizen wanted everyone around him to be upright. If you saw an opportunity to put some-body's life right, of course you should intervene. It was everyone's duty to intervene. (But other people interfering in your life, no way! It is good double-think, and reinforced now by democratic single-mindedness.)

That same day we had a wily Siberian up before us who pronounced his *a*'s like *o*'s and his *o*'s like *a*'s, and nobody at the Table could find a way of getting at him. I must have been in top form. I spotted his Achilles' heel but kept quiet for the time being. (During these manhunts I was not really a very big bad Wolf, my heart was not in it; although I could work up a frenzy with the best of them.) There seemed to be no way his judges could make him feel guilty (which is, after all, the main thing in any hearing). Time was dragging desperately. The questions were all wide of the mark. I needed a cigarette. My stomach was beginning to rumble, and purely out of frustration, I suddenly pointed to his weak point, jabbed, and punctured it. He couldn't think up a covering lie fast enough. "Hold on, hold on!" He was still hoping to wriggle out of it, thinking up lies as he beat an orderly retreat, but by now the rest of them were on to him. The bilious Proletarian Firebrand rushed through the breach, and all the others after him. Now once again, newly inspired, they fired question after question at him, moving in for the kill. Our wily friend snivelled, and started pronouncing his *o*'s like *o*'s and his *a*'s like *a*'s in a perfectly ordinary, if distraught, Moscow accent. (Only then did the full, rapacious thrill of the hunt hit me. I remember distinctly thinking that what he was guilty of was just a piece of nonsense, the sort of crap you find in every life. Why punish him for this piece of nonsense when what you really wanted was to punish him for the whole way he lived his life.)

There was another case after his that day, a woman. She was a fundamentally sad person, and she wept. Women nearly always did weep (but we knew their game). She was given a drink of water and time to pull herself together. The water continued swirling hypnotically in the decanter for some time afterwards. When her tears died down and she was again capable of answering intelligibly, we questioned her, and only then did our grilling make her feel properly guilty, her tears become unfeigned, and her hysterics the real thing.

That same evening (without of course being aware of the metaphysical imperative to engender new life) you left the tribunal with the Almost Pretty Woman, escorting her home; and drunk with the day's socializing, you both discussed loudly who had spoken how, and who had been done over in which way. Oh, of course the words you used were "discussed" and "investigated". You walked with her towards the metro, holding her arm and knowing (remembering) what she had said about her husband being away on business. You did not even ask whether you might accompany her, you simply went with her (and after her), shadowing her, pressuring her with all your youthful lupine energy. Within half an hour, somewhere up on the eighth floor of a prestigious and attractive apartment block, in a room well away from the front door (just in case), on an ottoman with a Bukhara rug hanging on the wall above it, she was yipping and squealing faintly in your arms. In those years moaning and shrieking had yet to become fashionable; the norm was a muted squealing which conveyed the message, "I feel you, I am responding to you, you are in me and I am all yours."

There were, I suppose, only three of them not susceptible to tribunal-induced randiness. Firstly, the Wise Old Man.

Secondly, that coarse old bag who always sat unspeaking in the furthermost left-hand corner of the Table (but not at the head, which was reserved for the Party Man). As an aid to memory I call that woman with her vulgar voice the Sales Assistant from the Corner Grocery, although she might have been from the market or worked at the regional vegetable distribution centre, or in a chain of street stalls. In rude health, and endowed beyond measure with body fat, she sat hour after hour at the tribunal Table looking inscrutable. She was there solely in order to be counted as having done her bit for the community. When she got caught stealing from her grocery or her vegetable centre, her hours of sitting at the Table would count in her favour. ("A community activist. Leave her alone.") She was no more than a shadow cast on those sitting next to her, on the red baize between them, and on the decanter. That was the only reason she was there. She almost never spoke, never smiled, never got angry. Sometimes she managed to say, "Uh-huh"; and the minute there was a proposal for a reprimand or a punishment, she raised her hand unhurriedly but firmly. She was in favour.

Equally immune from sex is the Grey-haired Woman in Spectacles. She is sympathetically disposed towards me from the outset (as she is towards anyone who is being called to account): she is only too familiar with the sensation of being a victim from her own life, or possibly from that of her son or daughter. She well understands the true nature of the tribunal, and knows how it feels when everybody is "in favour". Counteracting this, however, she knows that everybody knows about her *a priori* soft-heartedness and her predisposition to forgive, her inclination to understand, to turn a blind eye and save a victim from excessive humiliation. (She knows everybody knows, and keeps her feelings in check.)

She speaks a little brusquely (fearing to be accused of floweriness) and always seems incredibly meticulous: "Tell us, please, about the timescale of your actions. Or did everything come upon you at once, like a snowball?" Even here she is trying unobtrusively to help you out, suggesting alternatives, even though her voice is strict. And when they are wringing recantation out of a body and he is ready to go down on his knees and howl and beg for mercy, she is prepared to beg by his side. But without emotion. She will suddenly take off her spectacles, as if she is going to wipe the lenses with her handkerchief. She can no longer see you. You are lost in a vague white blur, like a blurry white mist (somewhere on the English coast; and if you are far away in England, they can't hurt you so much).

"Vitali, remind us of the regulation," she says, taking her spectacles off and not allowing herself to cry. (Vitali is the squeaky clean Taker of Minutes in the white shirt, the Secretarial Type.) He will, of course, remind us of anything he is told to. He must. Without asking why. (This means that, while he is leafing through his papers and reading from one of them the victim can enjoy a brief respite.) Her voice is actually rather imperious. Admittedly she is only being imperious towards the sleeked down and squeaky clean little Secretary rather than towards the victim (you). Nevertheless, her voice is strict. She is participating strictly and authoritatively, as none of the judges seated here can deny. Nobody can mutter the deservedly renowned reproach, "Always siding with your own lot!" A reproach which could be justified, because you are one of her own lot in spirit, kith and kin of all the world's victims.

When the hearing is over and everybody is heading off, the Grey-haired Woman in Spectacles feels wretched about not having been able to help you. (Most of the judges, as we know, will be feeling randy and heading off to procreate.) She is heading off to mourn. She kept her emotions to herself when you were being pecked and battered. (She is a bit of a coward. She knows that.) Now her emotions have been stirred and will gnaw at her for a long time.

That dim-witted fellow, the Proletarian Firebrand, also seems not to be affected by sexual urges during the questioning. (His passions seethe in other spheres. His peatbog burns on different levels.) For all that, the tribunal does provoke a delayed sexual response which ripens in him slowly. (I really can't see him clearly. His age is variable and so, consequently, is his physical appearance, but most probably his name is Piotr Ivanovich, and he is a stringy fellow with high cheek bones; his hair is wiry and encroaches on his low brow; and he wears a flat hat. I have no doubt he can scent people from a distance.)

Along with others he hurled himself at a man of educated appearance who was trying to sneak to the front of a line waiting for butter. At first, when everyone started shouting, he actually stood up for him, but then something in his psyche flipped and he went for the wimp's scraggy throat, while others were pummelling the malingerer. Pummel, pummel, pummel. The scrawny intellectual fell down, the police rushed up blowing their whistles, and everybody else promptly broke and ran for it. Only he, Piotr Ivanovich, stayed where he was. The intellectual himself jumped up, took to his heels without so much as a backward glance, and melted into the crowd (much the safest course in the circumstances). Stout Piotr Ivanovich stood his ground. What had occurred was so much the thing that gave meaning to his life, so much a moment of outpouring of his soul, that to have run away would have been tantamount to thrice denying himself. No coward, indeed courageous in his own way, he waited for the police. He was breathing heavily, and made no excuse.

(Although in fact he hadn't even hit the guy, only gone for his throat.)

He wants you to stand revealed before the Table of judgement as a totally useless prat whose nonentity will sooner or later bring you to that moral boundary beyond which nothing is sacred. He wants this established (shown up by the questioning as if on an X-ray), and then he wants you sent out to the fields. Let him dig trenches! Do manual labour! (No, not until he is half dead. We are not the Chinese. Just pack him off to some perfectly ordinary unmodernized factory to find out what real grafting is. And to eat the same food as other manual labourers, not always hot but always foul, the same food as bent him double many years ago and gave him his ulcer. Let the prat munch his way through that food without losing heart, and do a bit of thinking. Let him at the same time breathe the yellow fumes, sometimes even red but streaked with yellow, which belch out of the chimney round the clock.) But trench digging would be better. No beating it. A long trench stretching as far as the eye can see, dug out with a pick and shovel, and all you know is how tense your muscles are, and how with each swing of your arms another bit of your life has disappeared never to be seen again. (At the Table of judgement the Proletarian Firebrand is always passionately biased. He makes no attempt to conceal it. If anybody tries to give you an easy ride, they too will incur his untamable fury.)

After the tribunal he does not know what to do with himself. Having been seated all that time at the Table he doesn't feel like travelling by public transport. He walks part of the way home, and on the way it is somehow self-evident that he will perform good works, helping an old lady to cross the road, helping some plodder to carry his massively heavy suitcase to the metro, getting amicably out of the way for someone in a hurry. "Life is hard, but we'll tough it out, eh lads? We're not such a bad lot," he thinks. "Our city may be plain, but we love it. There's a lot of work yet to be done..."

As he walks through his native town his eyes mist over and he is intoxicated by the joy of living. It is only when he is almost home that the true, hidden nature of the tribunal suddenly catches up with him. He does not, of course, put two and two together, he merely finds that he is suddenly aflame with sexual desire. He is a simple man, and decides there and then that it must be too long since he last undertook a certain agreeable family obligation. He hurries home at top speed. He is no sooner in the door than, having barely had time to wash his hands, he hurls his wife on the double ottoman. "You've gone bananas. We haven't even had our little drink," she says grunting indignantly. "Screw the little drink! It's only your business-travel lovers who drink before they do it. To get it up. A red-blooded man doesn't need it!" he laughs. (He'll get well and truly plastered afterwards.)

Get rid of your own guilt feelings (by projecting them on to other people!). In my dealings with the tribunal there is a part of me which longs to sidestep the need for words and leap right out on to the red baize on their Table, there to weep a lake of tears. This puddle would, no doubt, start seeping over under the decanter and the One Who Asks the Questions, sitting near it, would start looking out of the side of his eye to see whether the decanter was cracked. (The Secretary and Taker of Minutes would not need to look: he knows there is no crack.) Perhaps I should let this puddle of tears come splashing out right now, in the night, ahead of time? There's a thought: I could let all my guilt pour out in advance (perhaps that's what's behind my insomnia!). Then when day dawns and I am called in the morning, I shall be ready to face my Talk without trickery or subterfuge. I came, I saw, I spilled the beans!

I can think of nothing to do in the kitchen. I light the gas. The little blue flame shows evenly above the burner. Put the kettle on again? It isn't tea I need. I need sleep.

There are crumbs on the kitchen table, so I must have had some tea after the valerian, with that stale gingerbread. I can't remember now. (Or how many pills I took. I didn't count. I can't remember.) My head aches the moment it touches the pillow. The pressure in my head increases when I lie down (in accordance with the laws of physics). The pain becomes frisky, it shrieks and squeals, but I can't make my mind up whether to take another pill, the next pill, that is. The last one may not have had its full effect yet (and I don't want to lower my blood pressure too much).

There are crumbs on the kitchen table. I look at them. But is this night table real, with its stale gingerbread crumbs?

The other Table is real. It is not just in my mind, an *idée fixe*. It is alive. As alive as a real night mountain, like twin-peaked Elbrus, with its left-hand and right-hand sections, which you cannot see at this moment but which is, of course, still there in the Northern Caucasus, where it always has been. It is there all right, with its snowy peaks.

(Perhaps I should wake my wife? I feel awful.)

My guilt feelings are more real than I am now. They have more reality than I and my relations with my wife and all those dearest to me. They have been beaten into me. I have been brainwashed, and when I peer into them it is just too dark. Circles of darkness.

Fear Is a Good Thing. The End of Fear Is the End of Life. Fear is only a form of life, something that makes it work. We should not speak ill of fear...

I feel ill. Fear is pushing me to seek company, but if I waken my wife or my daughter everyone will again be running from room to room, looking for pills, all that night-time bother. (They will be fussing for ages, like over a patient in hospital. I do not want to lie down and have people standing by my bedside asking me how I feel and trying to keep me calm. I really shall feel bad then; and have that lump in my throat.)

I could go into my wife's room right now and just lie down there on the edge of her bed without touching her (it's a wide bed), just knowing that she is alive and there. That would be enough. It would be enough for me too to sit on a chair, listening to her breathing, but I know that the moment I open the door she will wake up and start worrying. If only she would stay asleep!

When I was a little boy I woke up once in the middle of the night (with something disturbing me) and suddenly wanted to be near my mother, to see her and talk to her, but she was asleep. I hadn't the courage to go in and wake her up. The door was closed and, after a moment's hesitation, I lay down beside it and slipped just my little fingers under the door into her room. My fingers were in the room with her and that was enough for me. As soon as my fingers and half my hand were in there, my heart began beating evenly again and I breathed easily. (The sweetness of sleep clouded my frail young mind and stilled it.) That was how I fell asleep. I was wakened in the very early hours of the morning by a snow-laden wind which had blown up strongly in the night (bringing the first snow of far off nineteen forty-something...).

Pathetic *homo sovieticus.* I always think someone is to blame.

"You said you had to go to great lengths to find a cooperative apartment in order to get your son a separate place to live. Suddenly, in three months from start to finish, you fixed it. How come?"

The question is being asked by the One Who Asks the Questions. He has a high forehead and male-pattern balding.

"How did you get that apartment? I was sitting on all the relevant commissions of the Executive Committee, so clearly you must have found a way of avoiding that route. How?"

I am silent. I gave a bribe, that's how. To a self-important bureaucrat just like him. He was going bald too, and asked questions hastily. (Odd that he should be the one to ask. Or perhaps not. *I gave it to you.*)

"Perhaps you gave someone a bribe?" he asks, suggesting the unthinkable, and I can't resist giving myself a modest pleasure.

"Perhaps I did!"

"What? Surely not!" Consternation from every side. Now they are on to something wildly exciting.

This is immediately followed by Questions

bellowing:

"Do you know what you are saying? We shall go through the records for that year and arraign you on a charge of bribery!"

Of course, I take fright. (Pleasures always have to be paid for.)

"No, I don't remember... I only..."

"I don't remember! I don't remember," the Young Wolf Who Is Dangerous mimics. "He doesn't remember! We are all up to our eyeballs in work, but we can remember that we're here to listen to what you have to say. Who do you think you are? Do you think we have time to waste?"

"I don't think anything," I reply mechanically.

The Pretty Woman remarks quietly, but succinctly:

"Well, you should."

She just wants to say something. She is trying to be witty. I don't blame her. I am just trying to get out of trouble myself.

Turning up facts is really not what they are interested in. They get their kicks from turning up souls, and until a person has opened up and spilled his guts out in front of them they don't feel fulfilled. Concealment of facts irritates them, of course. (They don't need your secrets, but you must be made to hand them over anyway.)

Chapter 6

The extent to which they possess your soul is in inverse proportion to the extent to which they possess your body. The less they have your body, the more they want your defendant soul.

Take the example of a soldier guilty of some offence in olden times. Setting little store by his body (but keeping his soul very much to himself), he would cry out: "Shoot me, brothers! Shoot me, worthless louse that I am!" and crawl on the ground imploring them to shoot him. And some officer (not overly interested in his soul) would agree. "Yes. Fine. Go ahead. Shoot the louse!" The firing squad would form, raise their muskets, and nothing in the scene would be remotely reminiscent of the Table with the decanter, except that the poor sod might ask permission to drink himself silly one last time, and who could refuse him that?

The Era of the Cellars did involve interrogation, and since they were laying claim to part of your soul, they had correspondingly to forego part of the claim to your body. They could no longer just wordlessly put you up against a wall without interrogating you first, which is why the Cellar made its appearance, where you could be questioned and where it was also more convenient to sluice away all the accompanying fluids, blood from a broken nose, mucus or whatever. A prospective victim might piss himself in anticipation of the torture, or when he glimpsed the array of instruments. It could be seen

as a ploy, trying to part with this body fluid instead
of his soul, trying to get off lightly. (It eased the
interrogation, and the flagstones on the floor could
be swabbed over in no time at all by an old woman
or a fellow-prisoner, who might initially suppose he
had only been brought here to wash the floor and
get rid of the smell.)

It was already necessary at this time to go to
some lengths with the guilty party and pry into his
soul. He would resist. You had to start investigating
things he had said, ambiguous or potentially
blameworthy things he had done. At first he would
be amazed, and later horrified, at his own ambigui-
ties and would gradually come round to admitting
that, yes, that did happen, yes, I am an Enemy of
the People. Pain helped him to see things clearly
(by reducing the scope for self-deception). One of
the relatives of Party leader Nikolai Bukharin was
himself persecuted after the famous 1938 show trial.
He tells us: "The thing that amazed me about the
torture cellars of those years, which everybody
knows about nowadays, was the prevailing sense of
everyday routine. The torturers into whose hands
you had fallen had their beds in the same room,
some of them neatly made. One of them would
carry on sitting there, working away with needle and
thread while you were being beaten, only occasionally looking up when you screamed, and then
getting on with his darning. It was like a primitive
workshop, except of course for the screams of the
victim, whose teeth, mouth and nose were battered
and bleeding almost immediately. I noticed a
handsome young man there. He was on his way to
meet someone and he was late. He glanced at

himself in the mirror, straightened his peaked cap, and hurriedly explained to his colleagues, who didn't pause in the beating they were administering, 'I must fly, I really must. I'll put in some overtime later'."

During the Era of the White Coats those sitting in judgement got even less of your body. It hardly belonged to them at all. They got to swab your vein with cotton wool immediately before the injection and to call in a male nurse to twist your arms behind your back and restrain you. That was about the extent of it.

Your mind and soul, on the other hand, were almost wholly in their power and under their control. They justified their intervention in your cerebral cortex on the grounds of mental illness, and left you reacting very little to anything apart, of course, from the sudden bird phobia. Even that passed. The dissident was turned into a docile animal, a child. He ate and drank, and when they occasionally showed films he would ask, "Is it about the war?" the way a backward child might do.

The old Table with its baize covering was particularly sensitive to contact with the cool bottom of the decanter. (Damp circles would soak through the baize to the smooth table surface and dry out only gradually.)

The evolutionary process has culminated in those who ask the questions no longer having any claims on your body at all (not even in the form of injections, not even in the form of supplementing the diet of your brain). Your soul, on the other hand, is all theirs. The grilling I face tomorrow is by people who will probe the recesses of my soul because that is all that is left to them.

My arms, my legs, the rest of my body are out of bounds. They can neither fire bullets into me, nor whip me with a knout, nor even give me a course of Alionka. All they have left is to pry into my soul. Well, good luck to them. I hope they enjoy themselves.

They will open up your self, pull it apart, expose it to the last shred until there is nothing there but a blank sheet of paper, till they know its every twist and turn, till they have destroyed your personality...

I once knew a woman who, at the thought of being quizzed the next day by one of these little kangaroo courts of ours, would roll up into the foetal position and emit a thin wailing. Then she felt better and could sit down by the telephone for a chat with a friend and further relax her vulnerable soul. (She did not turn to relatives or close family. She would simply tell them not to worry about her. "Just let me have my wail.")

I know the hearings change my personality too (although not enough to make me start wailing). I know people whose whole appearance, down to the colour of their eyes, changes when they are due for a talk. You would not recognize the way they speak, the way they walk, the expression of the folds of their mouth, their whole temperament. Is it any wonder that under such circumstances people sometimes sell their friends short, or betray and cheat people they undoubtedly love. It is as if somebody else were doing it.

During this sleepless night I go over to the dark

window. I do not know what I am hoping for or what I want. I have persuaded myself that those seated at the Table are just another life form, that tomorrow's interrogation is a lot of silly nonsense (but have still not quite managed to shake off my guilt feelings).

If I do get over-excited and die on some such absurd night as this, I know the sin I shall beg God to forgive (if I am granted the time, and if He asks me). Yes, I was just like everyone else. Yes, they indoctrinated me; but even after I had intellectually outgrown all that, I (and my intellect) failed to make the leap out of the myths and structures of Soviet life. I lived by Soviet values. I did not manage to free even one foot. But I shall beg forgiveness (and take the blame) only for having accepted an earthly tribunal in place of the judgement of heaven.

I feel like making my way in the middle of the night to the modest executive committee of our regional Soviet (where I am to be questioned tomorrow). I feel like going in, giving the disabled watchman a half bottle of vodka, and going to take a look at the Table when it hasn't got people seated at it. I feel like touching it with my hand and asking it straight out,

"All right. What is it you want from me?"

It is night. I cannot sleep. Seeking someone to pass the buck to, my brain honestly toils on through the night. Trying to see the Table in the perspective of history, as I have been trained to in lessons of Marxism-Leninism, I push back in time to the Table of the Era of the Labour Camps with its official tribunal greyness, and then (even deeper) to the notorious quasi-judicial triumvirates, the troikas, and the Revolutionary Tribunals of the Civil War years where only three or four figures were seated at the Table. They were very brief and you said nothing. You said nothing because you were no longer you (you had "laid down your arms before the Party"), and because there was little hope: virtually none. The weight of the roof timbers seems to press down on you. It is an official log hut. There is a stove with firewood blazing and crackling in it. The One Who Asks the Questions glances towards the flames from time to time. They are seated, but there is no decanter. There is, however, an old-fashioned dark-coloured kettle with a long swan's neck spout out of which they top up their heavy glass tumblers with an even stream of tea. There are no teacups. They gulp the tea out of the glasses, scalding their throats, and then in comes the Pretty Woman (or Almost Pretty Woman) in her Bolshevik leather jacket. She wears an army shirt under the leather jacket and is too warm. She says,

"It's hot in here... You've really stoked up that stove!"

My thoughts go back further, stumbling upon individual figures from the obscurity of distant times, until from the late 1860s there finally emerges a revolutionary, Sergei Nechaev, none other than the prototype hero of Dostoevski's *The Devils.* (I could go even further back in time, but my thoughts pause here, clutching at Nechaev because he is the first person who looks as though he might plausibly be blamed for my misfortunes.) I blame him. His Group of Five is so archetypally close to all our later commissions and tribunals. Nechaev's Five have a special place in our intellectual history. This was the moment when conscience was delegated to the collective, and divine retribution entrusted to a group of human beings. Nechaev's co-conspirators took it upon themselves to weigh the life of an independent-minded student called Ivanov, found it wanting and, by killing him, said on our collective behalf, "Vengeance is ours; we will repay".

Nechaev was incarcerated to the end of his days in the Peter and Paul fortress in St Petersburg (in solitary confinement). There are no two ways about whether or not he knew he had ushered in a new historical era by instituting extra-judicial killing under collective responsibility. He knew all right (and was unrepentant).

In our own days, if you did not want to open up and spill your guts out to Them, like a pocket turned inside out, this was taken as a sign that you had turned in on yourself and did not wish to be open with the collective and the Soviet People. The equating of Them with the Soviet People was of Their devising. (I know you can read all this in any Russian newspaper nowadays. I just want to get it off my chest.)

Well, fair enough. Let all my life be just an ugly epiphenomenon of post-Nechaev history. Here I am in the middle of a sleepless night, my fingers blue from boiling up valerian root, having already measured out my two spoonfuls of the drops and readied a tablet of Clofilin just in case. On the one hand: me, quaking over tomorrow's absurd summons; and on the other: Superman Nechaev. Yet that is precisely where We have our origins, delegating conscience and the safeguarding of our souls to a group. ("The Party is always right," that clever man, Nikolai Bukharin, said in his moment of tragedy.) *They* are always right. Have you really liberated yourself of all that? Don't make me laugh. Tomorrow morning you are to go and explain yourself to perfectly ordinary folk who have only to say "We" to scare you witless. Tomorrow you will try to explain yourself and make excuses, in spite of all the explaining you have already done in the course of your long life. (Has that really not been enough?) Your heart is thumping. You have cardiac intermissions, that extra systole after the second beat is dangerous, I know. There are the telltale beads of sweat on my forehead. Listening to the beats, I count off the contractions of my heart like drops from a tap. Has the water all leaked out? That is the question. A double drop drips, splish-splash. Another drop, splash. Then suddenly, stop: the drop lingers, hanging, and there is no beat. The drop hangs there but it does not fall. There is no water left.

What did Nechaev feel during those ten years in solitary confinement? I send him greetings across a hundred years, from my night to his; from my Table to yours, Mr Nechaev. As the Idea gutters to its end (it is defunct) millions of pathetic former Soviet citizens, and I among them, are still trembling at the thought of our sad little post-Nechaev kangaroo courts. We still feel in our genes that perfunctory historic judgement of your fighting Five. I am not blaming you in the least. Apportioning blame is difficult and too much like hard work. (I just want to offload everything on to your shoulders.) *Homo sapiens*, that modest pygmy of history, wants nothing better before going to face a perfectly ordinary inquisition the next day than to be left in peace, and perhaps get a little sleep. Not blame: just sleep. I knew from the start that I was not really interested in finding someone to blame. Through heavy layers of time I am simply taking a human interest, and perhaps fancy saying something to him as if we had known each other for ages. "How did you sleep, Sergei old pal, in that solitary cell of yours? Did you pace up and down all night? How did you get on without valerian? Did you take your pulse? Did you have cardiac intermissions?"

It is so convenient to blame him, Them for everything (and I have every intention of doing so). As night approaches I need someone to blame. "Damn their eyes," I rage at the bolsheviks of all times, although all I need is for them to "claim" responsibility for my night fears and then I shall be able to get some sleep (even just a little). I dare say it is not Nechaev or other revolutionaries who ultimately carry the can, although they did bring matters to quite a pitch. But if it is not them, who is ultimately responsible? I can only point the finger at our ancient Russian commune, the *obshchina* (but let us leave that, at least, sacrosanct). Or perhaps this whole psychology of questioning and answering goes back even beyond the *obshchina* and is rooted in the dark plasma of primal human relationships...

I can't remember a different time. I have probably never lived outside this sense of guilt. At least, even in my moments of greatest awareness, I cannot remember what I was like before being socially engineered, any more than I can remember my earliest childhood. In the deep depths of my infancy there is an abyss of chaos like swirling water, dark and nebulous (there is no looking down into it now, no way of seeing). A changeful playing of darkness and light, a gleaming, a muffled sound (like something crunching under someone's quiet steps). These things rise from a deep well up to the conscious mind of my present-day self. They are no longer meant for me, or even my subconscious; and yet they are part of my self. The muffled sounds from down there are like crunching pebbles of my unquantifiable guilt. That is as much as I know about myself.

A cove had formed near the River Ural, horse-shoe shaped and quite large (not part of an old riverbed, just a cove). This was when I was a boy.

We once found a table there (which some men had brought on a truck for an open-air celebration and then gone off again, leaving it behind). The table lay there, exposed to the rain and the crows' droppings, until we boys turned it over and launched it on the water like an unconventional four-masted ship. We paddled with our hands, and our funny old tub sailed around the cove. We found an abandoned tablecloth (from the same celebration), and naturally made it into a sail, and tore a bit off for a flag (red, of course) for one of the front legs. Flying the red flag and shouting with glee we sailed our tub around the cove.

One time there was a storm, and the wind and rain drove the waves of the Ural up against our sandbar so that the mirror-like water of our cove almost joined up with the river. (We sat soaking in a lean-to, while our old tub circled the cove of its own accord, and Vovik Ryzhkov said worriedly, "Isn't it going to get carried out into the river?" "That's what it's supposed to do, dummy!" we shouted.) There was still just not quite enough water for us to give the upturned table a shove and sail off down the River Ural. Our ship would have sailed far, far away, and we all hoped fervently that the water would rise after the downpour, and we would set off on a great voyage.

Chapter 7

The Ordinary-looking Woman does in some elusive way also remind you of a secondary school mistress. She is the only one of the judges who sometimes sits on your side of the Table, probably because she is late. In fact probably she quite often fails to turn up to tribunals at all because of school or private commitments, which would explain why there is some uncertainty about where she is supposed to sit, as if officialdom hasn't got round to allocating her a place. She has an affected voice in which notes of pathos vie with tones of nobility.

"But where is justice," she cries aloud, projecting her trained schoolteacher's voice. "If we are to make demands of him, must we not equally demand justice from ourselves?"

An inner cautiousness (born of the knowledge that her position on the margins of the Table may rule out the possibility of lengthy deliberation) prevents her bringing out all the philosophical considerations pertinent to shortcomings in any life (including yours), but she will certainly draw attention to hidden emotional agendas. The facts will be relegated to the background while she urges a "level emotional playing-field".

Needless to say, she hopes that her intervention will be properly appreciated by the humiliated victim, namely you. She hopes there will be a condign appreciation of the sensitivity and special (feminine) fairness of what she has said. She hopes you will come up after the hearing or after her impassioned speech, in the interval, (failing which, she may come over to you herself) and say, "Your speech was so apposite. You feel my pain more deeply than others."

In her dreams (the fantasies of her upright soul) she would like the tribunal to last for as long as possible, and she would like you to come over to her after each of her interventions full of a sense of gratitude and common cause. It really doesn't matter if you are old or ugly (absolutely anything can be corrected in a fantasy). She wants to connect with you. (She wants, even in the middle of the tribunal, for there to be real human feelings, passion. So little comes one's way in real life.)

Her social intercourse with you during the intervals does not prevent her from demanding severe punishment for you at the conclusion of the investigation. That is her little paradox. Delving avidly into your state of mind, she urges all the others seated round the Table to understand you and your life: yet a bare hour later she has done a U-turn and is demanding your scalp, yielding in severity, perhaps, only to the Proletarian Firebrand and the Party Man. At this point the resemblance, both in her expression and her diction, to an ageing schoolmistress is particularly apparent. She speaks ardently in your defence even as she rejects you as a person (supposing that the paradox will convey a due sense of the profundity of her contribution to those present). Her comments are trenchant (and occasionally profound).

Although she would never admit it, what she would really like is to cast convention to the winds and be intimate with the man she is judging. (She would like, after a great emotional drama and a certain amount of soul-searching, for her to leave her husband and for you to leave your wife, and for the two of you to find each other spiritually and physically.) Redeemed or damned in the course of the tribunal (it does not much matter which), you and she would now be one. You would live in her apartment until, eventually, she grew disillusioned and recognized her mistake (as in the end she assuredly would). She would run around, bringing you cups of tea in the morning, before finally saying,

"What a disappointment you have turned out to be."

And turn her back on you.

The detail of turning her back on you is important. (Something to do with poetic justice.)

While speaking she occasionally drifts into sentimentality and starts feeling sorry for human-kind in general (bourgeois humane idealism). The next minute, however, she is back to crying out for justice and demanding punishment. She works herself up, switching between emotions and rocking your boat in the process, at one moment sincerely sympathetic towards you, the next sincerely demanding retribution.

Perhaps she is not actually quite so extreme (I may be being too harsh on her), and perhaps even in her dreams the great emotional drama would be cut, and the separation from her husband. She might just want (in her dreams) to invite you home, and in a kindly human way warm you, the accused.

Because she is too kindly for her own good, intimacy might well follow and only then, suddenly seeing the true situation, she would say, "My dear man," (not in anger, but condescendingly, with gentle reproof: "My dear *man*") "What a disappointment you have turned out to be."

And the following day, she would let matters between you and the Table and those seated at it take their course. She would see their point. Trying to be understanding only encourages the likes of you.

My own feelings towards this Ordinary-looking Woman who reminds me of a schoolmistress, are unusual and very mixed. I would not dare to try enlightening her about her real motivations, so terrifyingly visible is her nature to me, and so much do I fear touching her soul, weighed down as I am by the knowledge of my undoubted love for her. God will forgive me too.

There is another person I have an unusual relationship with (as indeed I have with myself). If things had been a bit different I could have become just like him. (This is why our residual resemblance, and our difference, are so complex.)

But where does he sit?

I sweep from right to left in my mind's eye: at the head of the table sits the Wise Old Man, followed by the whole of the team on the right-hand section of the Table: the Grey-haired Woman in Spectacles; then the Pretty Woman; the Young Wolf Who Is Dangerous; the Young Wolf Who Is Not Dangerous; and the Secretary and Taker of Minutes. (This brings us to the middle. I see the little Secretarial Type through the decanter, silhouetted by it.) Moving on to the left-hand section: the first is the One Who Asks the Questions; then the Proletarian Firebrand... Stop! Stop! There is the problem. The person I haven't described (with whom I have a complex relationship) has only quite recently appeared at the Table. He is one of the new boys, and he takes his seat where he can. That is why I failed to place him immediately. (Running through them all just now was a waste of time.) The mystery man can be seated in any position except, of course, the head of the Table to the right, where the indomitable Wise Old Man sits. He is always the first to arrive (insomnia?), which means that no one else can steal his place.

The mystery man may be characterized as follows: the Honest (but Socialized) Intellectual. That "but" is, alas, an essential qualifier. In some instances he can be defined simply as the One Who Has Returned to Life, or even more simply as the Returnee (if he was exiled or disgraced in the Brezhnev years).

He is a militant. He is one of those people who do not doubt that if you do not keep a close eye on people they will very soon crawl back off into the swamps of political reaction. He rarely confides in anyone. While he was living his hard life and thinking his honest thoughts, many others were boozing and bonking, and managing to fix themselves a career and a good reputation in the process. And to get rich! He has it in for today's people, which is why, as he listens to the person being questioned, he pays such keen attention to his every slip of the tongue. (He knows about Freudian slips.) Then he joins in, in his slow drawl:

"But why should you think you deserved any better? You giggled away to yourself in private, while society... You demonstratively turned away from... You..."

His list of accusations lengthens. He is always polite, never over-familiar. Of course, his decency and honesty ensure that, when he finally does work out what is what, he will leap passionately to your defence, but it can be difficult to reverse the whole drift of one of these interrogations. When it comes to the vote, everybody else is in favour of condemning you, and only he proves to be against (and often insists on registering an awkward "minority view" in total isolation).

His own Table, at which he will sit in judgement on you from time to time, extends over the entire city. It is a virtual Table many miles in length. Such distances can be tamed only by technology, in this case, the steam telephone. We are talking of the fabled city-wide Telephonic Table, at which he is particularly renowned for his directness and honesty.

He is vaguely aware that within his breast there lives a (partly) recycled Bolshevik. He is after all militant not because he is honest and direct, but honest and direct because he is militant. This initial cause generates a spiritual malaise in him of which he is aware. He suspects, indeed knows, that a persistent poison has built up in him, and looks round at all of us with disbelief, as if to say, "If even I am infected, what state must you scum be in?"

With his compressed energy he sets the tone

among the worthiest members of the intelligentsia, and before you know it Russia's finest sons and daughters, intelligent and decent, are busily dissecting you and the way you live your life from this Table which extends (from one apartment to another) the length and breadth of the city, through the massive prefabricated apartment blocks of the residential regions. The ends of this virtual Telephonic Table may be out of sight and undemarcated, but a Table is a Table, with a head to its right-hand section at which, in conformity with tradition, there sits its highly educated Wise Old Man, then its Grey-haired Woman in Spectacles, after her the Almost Pretty Woman, and then the two, but possibly more than two, Young Intellectuals (whom we shall refrain from calling Wolves).

"... He (i.e. you) didn't speak at the meeting: he did not even show. N.N. considers that he got the wind up, just plain chickened out," says the Young Intellectual.

The Wise Old Man says nothing. As we know, the Wise Old Man is slow to condemn.

"He (i.e. you) is trying to play safe," the Young Intellectual (we omit the word Wolf) continues down the telephone.

"Did N.N. say that? Are you sure?"

"N.N. phoned me."

"Yesterday?"

"Today. N.N. can see straight through people."

N.N., of course, is our friend the Returnee, a.k.a. the Honest (but Socialized) Intellectual.

The Wise Old Man thinks for a moment, before opining,

"There can be serious reasons... He (that is,

you) said he was ill."

"Exactly. He said."

The Wise Old Man says nothing.

"If tomorrow you or I found ourselves caught by the short and curlies" (the young man sees nothing out of the ordinary in addressing this figure of speech to the Wise Old Man), we would not start having second thoughts and saying we were ill. We would rush to the defence. We are ready any time. Isn't that right?"

In the heat of the moment they too often blurt out that "We". They no longer talk about "the Soviet People" or claim to speak in its name, but when you are accused in the name of this "We", and find yourself sitting utterly alone on this side of the Table, it still hurts. (You also feel that tugging at your heart, and the guilt, your indisputable guilt, and a kind of eternal wretched state of being *maudit*.)

"... It is essential to form public opinion. A rapid reaction public opinion. N.N. said that."

"You really can't just go blackening someone's name like that. You mustn't be in such a hurry to tarnish a reputation. You can't call someone's honour into question..." Even here the Grey-haired Woman in Spectacles speaks up for the defence, playing for time in the interests of the accused.

Oh, all right. Three people cannot take part in a telephone conference in Russia yet, but if with a little licence we were to bring together three, or even five or ten, telephone conversations, we could recreate the same familiar discussion at this virtual Table. (The intimacy of the telephone brings out every nuance of the pauses and things left unsaid at a conventional Table session.)

"Dear Anna Mikhailovna! God bless you! N.N. said that all these words, 'reputation', 'honour' and what have you, really don't fit the bill nowadays. We live in an era when there are no more political prisoners, but we still behave as if we were all still in the camps."

"I don't."

"You just think that! Don't dig your heels in. We really do need to phone Ostrogorski right away; and the best thing, Anna Mikhailovna, would be if you were the person to phone."

(The pressure is on again.) This unseen concerting of the judges is a special attribute of the Telephonic Table. Late at night people are sitting in their warm flats, out of sight of each other. The virtual city-wide Table has the additional attribute that, convened in these evening hours, you know nothing about it. It is convened (or assembled) behind your back. You are excluded. There comes a point, however, when you exert yourself and all your sensitivity, and suddenly go to great efforts to transform this virtual kangaroo court into reality. You will want it yourself. You (since nobody is going to summon you to a tribunal) will invite them all to join you at the Table (thinking up a reason for a get-together). You yourself will set out the bottles of Narzan water, perhaps even vodka, on the Table, yourself cover it with the cloth. You may even find yourself working out which of them should be seated where, not wholly trusting to their intimacy. And only at the end of the talk, as a joke, you may replace the bottles with a decanter, so that everything should be entirely proper. You yourself will have to sit down in front of all of them at the Table, making sure your eyes are sufficiently filled with penitence, and making sure too that at their first words you hang your head to one side in supplication: "Forgive me, friends, for I have sinned."

Even after that you will be plagued by guilt feelings for a time. As if still partly maculate and seeking absolution, you will now sign all their protests and open letters instantly, and speak and make declarations without thinking overlong what it is all about (lest, heaven forbid, you be detected in momentary hesitation or doubt). Such is the power of the Baize-covered Table with the Decanter in the Middle. Or, perhaps, such is the power of your personal susceptibility to being investigated at the Table. Or such, perhaps, is the powerful need which sinners themselves have of being judged. Who is to say?

"We are not trying to place you under any sort of compulsion over this. You are a free agent. If you can't agree to support us, we will continue to regard you precisely as we do now and our good opinion of you will not change," they say, the best sons and daughters of Russia. They aren't just saying it: they really believe it, they are sincere. (But, of course, they are not yet seated at the Table.)

In a conventional court (for dealing with robberies or assaults), you are brought in, they have a quick look in the Criminal Code, decide which article best fits the case, and slam you for however long it says. There's the article, so that's the sentence. Wallop!

Why should they start involving themselves in the detail of your long life if the offence is obvious and they can straightaway look up the punishment? "Aha, Citizen K? No problem. Subsection 152. Wallop!" In this respect the court is like an old postal worker who just sits there endlessly postmarking envelopes with a rubber stamp. They set the old man to do this job because they thought he was past anything more creative, so there he now sits stamping away. Sometimes he hits the right spot, sometimes he misses (wrong article, wrong sentence!), but he carries on thumping away at the envelopes in front of him (as if they were so many human destinies). Wallop! Wallop! Wallop!

A punishment decided absolves you instantly. Once I was walking down the street a bit "unsteady on my feet". A car turned so sharply it nearly ran me over. I angrily gave it a good kick in the side and, not surprisingly, dented it. The driver jumped out at the next corner and complained to the policeman on duty. They promptly pulled me in, of course, and until they could look into it, kept me at the police station all night, although they told me straightaway what fine I would get. It was pretty steep. I had every reason to be indignant, but instead I was almost elated sitting in their stinking custody cell. There I sat under lock and key in the stifling heat and wondering why on earth I was feeling so pleased with myself. The reason was simply that I already knew what the offence was going to cost me, which effectively purged my guilt, which meant I no longer felt guilty.

This is exactly the reason they are never in any

hurry to decide on a punishment for you. For them the main thing is the questioning. Once you've been punished you're off the hook. To all intents and purposes you're free, you can walk away, they've lost you. (I was back to thinking about tomorrow.) The criminal court concerns itself with a specific offence, whereas a tribunal battens on the whole of your life. In court you sit in the dock or to one side on a chair, separate from the judges. You are your own man. But if they move your chair nearer so that you end up sitting beside them at the same Table, you become somebody on the same side as them. Just moving you closer changes your situation from that of K (as Kafka called his hero at the beginning of the century) into that of someone close to them, the black sheep of the family. Whether you like it or not, you have no choice but to come clean to your family. "You are one of us. We are all completely on the same side. We are family," they say, and from that moment you can be sure of finding no forgiveness.

It is a known fact that people who believe in God do not turn themselves and their souls inside out for the benefit of these tribunals (which used to, and still does, make the judges very cross). It is not that they are especially stubborn or heroic. In a perfectly natural way, religious believers simply consider both the criminal court and any sub-variant of a tribunal to be an earthly court, and tailor their answers to accord with its relative unimportance.

They simply refuse to respond to many questions, replying that, "In this I am answerable only to God."

Often enough someone will come home from a tribunal and boast to his wife or friends, "I outwitted the lot of them! I tricked them! I pretended I was a complete idiot!" He tells exactly how he tricked them and how precisely he outwitted them, and all around laugh with great satisfaction.

He may have tricked them, but the investigation is not over. He may trick them one hundred and twenty-five times, only to be nailed the one hundred and twenty-sixth time. The tribunal is in no hurry. That is its strength. "What do you mean, dead? What did he die of?" "Stress. He died the evening before he was due up before the commission," the neighbours willingly tell you. So who tricks whom is something only time will tell. This particular team has been around for a long time. The fact that each of the judges has himself (on many occasions in his life) been subjected to precisely the same sort of questioning, makes not the slightest difference. The appearance and composition of the questioners is immutable.

While they wait to go in, the five people sit noticeably apart from one another. In silence. Nobody will ask anybody about anything. Each is enclosed in his own life (waiting to be questioned: not a good moment). Meanwhile, those on the other side of the door are seated at their long Table preparing to get on with the job. (Today they are on the other side of the process of humiliation.) If, however, for any reason their intention of fishing around up to their elbows in your life is frustrated, they will simply terminate the questioning. Amazing, but true! They will suddenly send you on your way in peace, as if agreeing that, "Well, these things happen. Off you go, now."

They had one old man practically hysterical, but then he stuck his finger up his nose and started pulling out a long green string of snot. They just let him leave. (He was pulling it out for an unbearably long time, practically winding it on to his hand.) When the team at the Table set about another disabled person too zealously, he got so disturbed he started farting: not loudly, but loudly enough so they couldn't pretend nothing was happening. Again they hastily let the old man go. This was minuted as, "the discussion became unproductive". The brevity of their questioning proved the saving of both these old men. (God, as is generally agreed in Russia, looks after the simple-hearted.) They were trying to drive the old men out of their homes to be resettled somewhere outside the city, "closer to the countryside". There were five of them who were very old indeed but who, despite their great age, still did not have all their documents (residence permit, right to accommodation) quite in order. Needless to say they were evicted, but before that they had of course to be quizzed about the entire course of their lives. Had they been in German captivity? Why had they left work in such-and-such a year? Why did they get on so badly with their neighbours? And so on and so forth, all of it leading to the simple and obvious conclusion that they were *guilty*.

As reported at the time, two of the five old men were so intimidated by their questioning that they died within a week of it. A third died of stress the day before the tribunal, but two survived, the same two, of course, whose questioning was aborted: the one who farted, and the one with the snotty nose.

The killer for the judges was not the anti-aesthetic aspect, but the fact that the person they were questioning did not have his soul keyed up to the occasion. They lost all desire to question him further. As skilled and thrusting as they were, they suddenly lost the urge.

I remember a not very sober citizen who hiccuped now and again as he sat on the chair staring at a point on the opposite wall. They had already had to call him twice: "Zapekanov? Is there a Zapekanov here?" but he just went on staring fixedly ahead. Only at the third call did he allow himself to be distracted from his reverie and went through to the room where they were all sitting ready to interrogate him. It was a famous occasion. The "drunk" bore himself fearlessly. He knew they could neither smell vodka on his breath, nor hold his reddened eyes against him today: he had drunk no vodka, merely sucked his way through two tubes of athlete's foot ointment.

The inquisitors knew from years of experience that a drunk (whatever the reason for calling him in) turns up to the tribunal sober (for the first time in months), and that was what they were expecting. The result is that he is even more depressed and miserable than usual, ready to agree about anything you care to mention, and quite likely even to cry. Zapekanov on this occasion, however, was rather jaunty and certainly not intimidated. (Having put away two tubes of ointment, his attempts at jokes were rather odd, but in any case no one was really expecting a great show of intellect from him.)

"I'd like to see half of you dead and buried," he quipped after every two questions in reply to the third. It was obviously pointless to continue the discussion. When one of those seated at the Table asked with heavy sarcasm, "In white slippers?" Zapekanov replied, continuing his train of thought,

"No. Barefoot."

They do not try rooting around in the soul of someone who is obviously different, a dwarf, say, or an albino, or somebody with an obvious physical disability. In fact they dry up instantly, the questioning grinds to a halt, and the dwarfs, albinos, or cripples depart virtually uninvestigated.

The same goes for stutterers and the mentally retarded. One way of evading a quizzing is to low like a cow before each of your responses. (A mere meditative "mm-yes," will not save you, it is too common.) What works well is to pronounce both vowels and consonants as lengthily as possible, with a marked drawl. "Mm-mmuh. I mmreally mmmmuh think..." But don't then go on to answer the question. Start again another time or two: "Mmmuh, I think mm-mmuh. I think mmm-muh..." relishing every sound. (Half measures will get you nowhere. You've got to really moo. It is not the humane instincts of the judges at their Table that you are activating but their sense of inadequacy (Glory be!) for the role of an all-seeing God. They have no lack of pretensions, but for all that they are cowards at heart. They know that God is in a different league, and have a superstitious dread of calling down His wrath upon their heads. So they release the halt and the lame to go about their business. They leave the handicapped in God's hands, as if to say, these are no concern of ours.

Everyone else, however, very much is their concern. Everyone else, of course, is in their hands.

It is night.

The time will come when I am very old and come to the last tribunal of my life. I shall sit down in front of my last Table (where, possibly, the matter under consideration will be my right to order a coffin. Possibly there will be major supply problems with coffins at the time, a shortage of boards, a shortage of nails... There was recently a report on the radio about some man having to be buried in a child's coffin. Such things happen. Their last investigation of my case will get under way. I arrive. They are seated. (Should he be allowed a coffin and, if so, how soon? Should he get it in advance, or should his wife be made to queue for it. There seems no reason why she shouldn't. His children too. Somebody at the Table is bound to point out that he has grown-up children.) Since I am not an albino, the investigation will be long and detailed. I shall have been worrying about it since the previous evening, sleeping badly during the night, trying to get my blood pressure down and taking valerian, but I'll be there on the dot in the morning.

They will be arranged round the Table and the decanter the same way they always are. The same people. They won't have aged a day, and will carry on talking among themselves as I come in. The squeaky clean little Secretarial Type and Taker of Minutes will say without a moment's hesitation, "Come in. Sit down..." To his left will be the Intellectual Who Asks the Questions, who will already be wondering what to start in with. To his left will be the unspeaking Sales Assistant from the Corner Grocery, still with the same seven years to go before she retires, and with the same puffy white hands. I cannot fail to notice the Pretty Woman, who will still have the same first wrinkles; and there will still be no trace of grey in the luxuriant locks of the Young Wolves sitting next to her.

The investigation will be long and difficult, but to some extent I shall feel better. Yes, this is how I was, yes, that is how I was, but now it is all over. This is the last time. I shall trade some terse remarks with my judges, but without getting angry in the least, and for the first time, perhaps, will have no feelings of guilt. What more could a man ask? What will be will be. What do I care if they decide not to issue me a coffin and my children ("They are full-grown adults, for heaven's sake!") have to run around tracking the wood down themselves. Never mind. Let it be. I have spent my life running around like a maniac. It is their turn now.

Chapter 8

The Honest (but Socialized) Intellectual does not really enjoy interrogating and tormenting people. Trampling on them yes, but even then only in moderation, only until the first tears come, until you are made to look pathetic, and crumpled rather than crushed. Then he wants you booted out as quickly as possible.

(My mind continues its searching. It is night.) What about that scraggy little fellow the Proletarian Firebrand? How is he going to jump? I'm sure his bad temper all stems from being treated badly. (Not like me, by phantoms in the night. Most likely it's been an accumulation of gibes and pinpricks during the hours of daylight.) Why don't he and I join forces? My eternal anxiety about the tribunal might tie in nicely with his eternal sense of being put down. He is, however, unpredictable. I once got talking to someone like that in a canteen (in those days canteens still sold wine by the glass). He would grumble away, and in the course of those noisy lunch-time half-hours I came round to seeing why he felt so hard done by. I humoured him, and did what I could to make him feel better. One time we had had a drink together and I had been sympathizing. We were getting on really well when he suddenly punched me in the face. He was sitting opposite, and just landed me one right between the eyes. For a moment I couldn't see a thing, only hear him swearing: "Bastards! They're all bastards! All just fucking bastards!"

With my night vision I can see straight through the Young Wolf Who Is Dangerous, where he is coming from and what makes him tick. The way he shakes hands with you! "Put it there!" he says, and a wide open smile ploughs through him to the bottom of his heart. He is generous. He will give you money; a place to live; a place to sleep; he will even, if you ask him, give you the money for a drink.

He finds the tribunal hard going. (You see him fidgeting sometimes.) After the tribunal he...

The whole point is, however, that they are as inseparable as the Table itself is indivisible. They are only Them when assembled together. Each of them taken individually is just as ordinary as I am, just as care-worn and, as if that wasn't enough, waiting just like me to be summoned every now and again to a talk at a Baize-covered Table with a Decanter in the Middle. Just like me (and perhaps even in the same week) one of them may find himself on the wrong side of the Table.

Tomorrow when I am under investigation, he will be one of Them; but the day after, perhaps even tomorrow evening, they will call him in to a different tribunal in a different connection, and then he will be Me.

The indivisibility of the Table (the inseparability of an individual questioner from all the others) is, of course, something I have known about for a long time, so why do I now waste time thinking about the possibility of making personal contact with one or other of them? (I can't help it. It is a night thought, there is no logic to it.) "Oh no you don't.

You've got to love not one of us, but all of us together, and at the same time," they say. In the middle of the night, crushed beneath a landslide of insomnia, I am prepared to do it. It seems to me to be within reach. (It is difficult to explain.)

This mixture of love and fear of them is very depressing. (If I could only build up a really virulent hatred of one of them, I should be filled with such self-respect.) I love them long before they start trampling, insulting and tormenting me with their crude, niggling questions. I love them in order to survive. I have had to learn to love them, because that is the only basis on which I can argue with them, dispute flexibly, flare up in disagreement, and curry favour.

It is important, essential even, for me to talk to them in my mind (and love them) before going to bed. If I don't I shall wake up in the morning in such a state. It is just the way I am. It is too late for me to change. (If I tried working myself up to a fury the night before, I would not wake up a valiant warrior. At best I should wake up hysterical, savage all who crossed my path, and might even suddenly overturn their Table and make all the bottles of mineral water crash to the floor. (The decanter would not crash to the floor. The Secretarial Type would catch it. Obviously.)

I did once try making contact with one of them in advance. I remember I boldly decided to drop in one evening for tea without so much as a preliminary phone call. Who to? It was the Intellectual One Who Asks the Questions. As I recall, he really did have a high forehead and male-pattern balding. His name was Ostroverkhov (Or Ostrolistov?). It seemed to me at the time that dropping in on him at home without warning the evening before the commission was highly original. I thought it would be very Russian. "I was just passing. Thought I might pop in for a moment. I am, understandably I think, a bit worried," I would say, and there would be a pause. Of course there would. I would have stopped talking. As if plucking my deepening silence out of the pause, he would start in himself. "There now, there now. Whatever is there to worry about! A routine investigation. It never occurred..." That sort of thing. "But why are we standing here, do come in. We have been having supper and were just about to have a cup of tea." He would not be saying this only from the goodness of his heart, but also because he would be a little taken aback. (I was even rather counting on that.)

It was amazing how right I got it! From the entrance hall I could see that there were in fact two women sitting in the kitchen, his family. I noticed their teacups (empty as yet), and heard the welcoming sound of a kettle coming to the boil on the stove. Ostrogradov, that was his name. Ostrogradov. Acquiring a surname (instead of just being the Intellectual One Who Asks the Questions) made him more human immediately. He did not say to me in the hall, "What exactly can I do for you?" There was nothing rude or offputting in his questions (indeed he did not ask any, indeed he was dumbstruck). He seemed to have no idea what to do: he dried up completely after his first few words. We both stood there in the hall, mute. I had, of course, quite correctly foreseen this pause, but it was going on for too long and beginning to jeopardize the impulsive Russianness of my coming to visit him. Our thoughts about each other suddenly got into a whirl of dangerous suppositions. "Has this person perhaps brought money in a plain envelope? God forbid! How did he find out my address?" "I hope he does not think I have brought him a bribe. I hope he isn't alarmed that I managed to find out his address."

We stood in silence some more. "I was just passing and thought I would pop in. That's all. I'll be off home now, then," I said finally (repeating what I had already said at the door, only now shifting from one foot to the other in the hallway). I was repeating myself, trying desperately to impart some clear expression to my face for him to read. For his part he was also doing his best, his face working. "Home?" he latched on to my last word, producing fortuitously, as sometimes happens, a kind of sense. He had not yet registered this, however, and a light show of emotional non-communication continued to run over his face. Now it was my turn to latch on to the word. "Yes, yes. Home. So... goodbye, then!" I said, for some reason rather grandly. I left. I could feel goose pimples on my back as he walked behind me, complaining. "Our elevator doesn't work properly. It really is too bad. It is a truly terrible elevator. They just don't seem to know how to repair it properly," he said as it rose irreproachably and I got into it. I left. He, of course, went back into his apartment and through to the kitchen, where the women were sitting with their cups of tea. There (I surmise), before explaining to them what *that* was all about, he took some time to recover his composure, while they looked at him in bewilderment.

When they are assembled together, their presence and their powers are in the Table. The thought, almost childish, has crossed my mind before of seating myself at the Table when there is nobody there. (Going there in the middle of the night.) Seating myself at their Table, and just sitting there for a time, cool and relaxed, and entirely alone. To prepare myself psychologically (and sap the Table of its metaphysical power) would certainly be worth doing, one point at least in my favour. Just to sit there with it, one to one, and let Them arrive later, after me, and take their seats, after me.

They would not know I had already been there, and seen the Table when it was simply a table, had already been seated at it (and mentally seated all of them in their places). The Table would be uncovered at night, I would see its cigarette burns, its cracks, the places where the varnish had come off. It was an old table.

This was something new in my hitherto rather unimaginative night excitements (I rehearsed the thought: now I am arriving...). It is night (neither night nor morning). A four-storey office block, a janitor at the entrance performing the office of security man. He would hardly prove much of a problem. "I left some of my papers in the committee room yesterday. We were sitting till late. I need them rather urgently." (Or should I stick to the traditional forgotten umbrella?) I would be looking suitably respectable, with a briefcase in my hand and a bottle of vodka in the briefcase in reserve. "Can't it wait till morning?" "It could, but I am afraid the cleaner may clear them away. She comes in very early." "I know she does," he grumbles. I produce the vodka.

"Here, my friend. Have this for your trouble..." They sell vodka at our local shop in hideous Fanta bottles. It looks terrible. (When I get home we pour the vodka out of the Fanta bottle into grandfather's old, cracked decanter. It makes an amazing musical sound if you accidentally clink it. A marked auditory contrast with that dull decanter full of water in the middle of the Table. But I'm being emotional.) Fanta bottles, despite the continuing irritation of their appearance, have proved with time to have compensating advantages. They make convenient presents or bribes; you can even drop them (they are unbreakable). They have the additional advantage of holding only a third, rather than a half, litre of vodka. (Just the right amount for the recipient to get through on his own, and more discreet. Security men cheerfully settle for a Fanta bottle rather than a full bottle.)

So, I slip him his third of a litre and go on in. It is early. The janitor will come up to the right floor with me, unlock the committee room door but not, of course, come in. He'll leave me to it. So there I am. There is the Table. I am not asking much, just three or four minutes to myself. I shall move a chair over and sit myself down. I can imagine the other chairs (and the judges too if I want to, but I shan't want to). What really matters is for me to put my hands down flat on the Table and just feel it: for two minutes, even one, but in silence, man to Table.

This is hardly likely to enable me to destroy the metaphysical powers of the Table (but I shall have moved closer to them). While I am sitting by the door waiting to be called in, the Table will also in some sense be waiting for me. It will remember my hands.

They will call one or other of those waiting, and somebody will go in before me, wiping the sweat from his face or nervously clearing his throat. I will be thinking to myself, what's he so worked up about? There's nothing special in there: just an old table.

The Table's surface will be cracked. It may possibly bear ancient marks from where tall candles from distant years have burned down to it. (I am imagining myself already seated at the Table, at night, alone.) The old Table will be completely exposed to me. I shall be able to stare at its splitting veneer as if peering into its long, long life. This time it will be I who will pry into its life (and put a few questions to it). I imagine how gently, how lovingly I shall run my hand over the surface, and how for a moment it will come to life, roused from the slumber of decades. There will be just the two of us. The old Table will feel the touch of my hand and, ever so slightly, shudder in response. It will return an answering warmth into my hand (with a barely perceptible sigh of centennial weariness).

The nights are quite dark at present. Will I switch the lights on? Probably I shall, although if I do go into the committee room I could easily find the Table even in the dark. I shall walk rapidly in the darkness to the middle of the room. The Table is always in the middle of the room. The first thing I shall do (even before gazing into it) is lay my hands on it, imparting my warmth to its old cracked surface.

I only once encountered the Proletarian Firebrand when he was being kind, in a genre picture. Twilight had already fallen. It was evening. (I was walking along a river bank, lost.) The forest was vast, the path obstructed by new growth, and at that very moment he jumped out from somewhere with an old-fashioned hurricane lantern in his hand. He quickly glanced at me, and said in a voice full of concern, "Anikeev, I am: Anikeev. Let's be gone from here. I will show you the way. I am Anikeev." He spoke simply, with no edge to his voice, and I felt that at heart he was a kind person. (It was just a pity that most of my encounters with him had not taken place in such natural circumstances as here, by the river.) He raised the lantern: "Let us be off..." He did not remind me again that his name was Anikeev, evidently satisfied that I would be remembering. He was right. Hearing his real name was important to me. (This detail, this transformation of the Proletarian Firebrand into someone who was just an ordinary human being, gave me a powerful sense of being able to trust him.) He raised the lantern, and in the undergrowth we found the entrance to a tunnel under the river. We went in, and the reddish light from the lantern ran on ahead of us along the tunnel walls. Underfoot too, points of light on the wet earth.

Chapter 9

The One Who Asks the Questions looks like a highly paid engineer. (This is because he is an engineer, intelligent, and working somewhere at a PO Box number now declassified.) He is tall and talkative, but when it is time to decide he invariably looks round at all of them. It is strange to see him indecisive, with his intelligence and his high fore-head, and his pleasing hands. The succession of questions he fires at you is a disguise. (If he falls silent, stops Asking Questions, tones down the passionate involvement, everybody will immediately see him for what he is: a Vacillating Intellectual.) Those questions are a channel he is not going to abandon, risking his true self and his shimmering water where the river is shallow and fast-flowing. Sensible man: he knows his limitations.

He is no longer very ambitious. (It is a long time since he was a Wolf.) His best years are behind him as he knows very well (but he still hangs on in there). Sometimes you can't understand what he has just said: he has suddenly Asked a Question so timidly and furtively you feel he is afraid of breaking the ice beneath you.

...She wears sweaters. They cling admirably to her bust which, in conformity with current fashion, is slightly pendulous but still decidedly pert. She is the Pretty Woman, but could only be given a wholly objective assessment if removed from her seat at the Table and viewed in a strictly everyday setting.

(Removing her from the Table would immediately detract from her a great deal. The Table with its decanter, the people, the investigation process really are her natural setting.)

It is night... sitting in the kitchen or wandering about the corridor, weary, sick with worry, you call her face to mind, her regular features, and suddenly (to your own surprise) tell her in the stillness of the night, "I love you, I love you. How can you not understand?" There is no doubting the seriousness of the words, or the consternation in your voice. Of course, it is all just crazy night fantasies.

The Wise Old Man is alarmed by the rate of never-ending change. He is fearful that his wisdom may not be keeping pace. He is even downright timorous. When he is at home he is a prey to moments of despair (and phones the Secretarial Type to ask him to dispel his fears. He does not say, "Dispel my fears." Instead he asks, "What do we have on the agenda for tomorrow?" or "What is happening about Zatravin? That case seems to be dragging on a bit." Or, "What is happening about Kliuchariov?" Further minor queries then arise, and he asks more and more questions.).

Sitting down at the Table of judgement with all the rest of them, he is immersed in himself and his long life (which also seems to be dragging on a bit). I, meanwhile, enchanted by his silence, imagine he is thinking about me.

One of the good things about my relations with the Wise Old Man is that he cannot sleep at night either. He is plagued by insomnia and, whether he feels like it or not, is bound to think about those whom he is judging tomorrow. He is just like the Grey-haired Woman in Spectacles, in that he and she are the two people who may spare a thought for me this night. Like all who despair and are unable to sleep, I shall inevitably at some point stand motionless by the window (the kitchen window, my night window) and with unseeing eyes look down at the night earth wet from rain (or the wet night snow) and suddenly say for no apparent reason, softly, "Lord God Al*mighty*..." Not because I am suddenly mindful of my Maker, but simply because of the stillness and a sense of depersonalized impotence. Almighty. The sound will break away from the word. The long vowel will spread through the night expanses breathing rain (or snow), and disperse in the night city until not a trace of it remains (and yet a trace will remain).

Both of them will stand transfixed for a moment as the lost sound reaches them, and no matter what thought next comes into their minds, it will have been a thought of me.

I know the Grey-haired Woman in Spectacles feels genuinely sorry for me, and knows that I understand her own state of mind. Our mutual pity makes no sense, but for all that we have a relationship. My opinion matters to her. She imagines that, since I understand her well, I shall have no difficulty forgiving her if she should suddenly be unable at the Table to resist the general chorus of condemnation and start singing along with them, switching sides. (In this she is over-optimistic. I shall forgive her, but not without difficulty.)

...although he has had to watch his step these last few years, he can still (if they let him) sum up the proceedings very well.

There is liking for you and openness in his face; and always that standard light grey suit a size or two larger than it should be. His tie is loosened, revealing a smooth white neck.

The Party Man is married to a very young student. (He gives lectures here and there. Why not?) We can be sure that she is very young and very slim, has little pink lips, and many, many erudite thoughts for which she is in his debt. She is the sort of girl for whom his authority and his attractive grey suit will never be undermined by any number of *perestroika*'s. She worships him. Her lips tremble when she wants to add a few words of her own to what he has said. (Is it any wonder that he now finds this more flattering than anything else in life?)

It is night.

"Why did you keep quiet about this? Do not imagine everybody else is stupid. We can see straight through you. You are transparent!" The former Party Man is wading into you. (The nearer the night comes to its culmination, the more personal your relations with them all become.)

You say,

"But listen! Wait! How could I have known in advance? Appreciate my actual situation. I am only human: put yourself in my shoes..." (This is for the Wise Old Man's benefit. He says nothing. He will assuredly put himself in my shoes and identify with me, only not yet.)

The Ordinary-looking Woman says,

"...he only thinks about himself. He thinks the sun rises and sets on himself. This egocentricity is more repugnant than the selective amnesia of an outright profligate. Forgive me, but this is just typical of our society!" She shouts the words out indignantly, this woman with the good ordinary face and the manners of a good honest schoolteacher. (She knows everything about what is typical of our society, both our types and their prototypes. The Wise Old Man is still saying nothing. Oh, do wake up, Wise Old Man...)

Their questions and my self-seeking night answers start my head burning again. My blood pressure shoots up, but I am in the thick of an argument. I go on and on answering them, and the more hostile and ill-natured the things they say, the more edgy and ill-natured are my answers.

You need, however, to answer in good time and coolly and to have planned ahead. It would be very tiresome if, not now during the night, but tomorrow after the questioning is over, I were to glimpse a spark which then burst dazzlingly but too late into the rejoinder they deserved. Oh how my heart would weep over this answer discovered too late; how I should berate my sluggish mind and futile tongue: "That's what I should have said. That's how I should have answered her (or him)," my soul would gibber too late, having been insulted and injured so cheaply during their questioning.

It is night. I look out the night window. (An

empty street, darkened windows in the apartments opposite.) I look behind me. Something stirs deep in my memory at the sight of my dozy old alarm clock. *A drum roll at dawn...*

...those people sitting there strengthened their position each time they entered my consciousness. (Their Table now stands on four hundred legs, oaken, massive.) They have strengthened their position with each successive questioning. They are part of me, unquestionably. They are alive. They probably represent the destruction of human identity. (Ten or twelve people always sitting inside you waiting to pull you up short.) I find it equally unpleasant to crumble with the passing years, and to have high blood pressure and a failing heart, and legs no longer firm, and having to take valerian in order to keep my nerves under control. When I think about encroaching infirmity, however, what is most unpleasant of all is that now I cannot even think of simply skipping tomorrow's questioning, just not going to see them. (I cannot not turn up to myself.)

Of course, it is healthy to recoil at the sight of ruined lives (but I try to be understanding towards myself. I am what I am!). I have noticed that I am sympathetic towards other people shipwrecked by life. I accept them. I have a pre-disposition to share in their misfortune, the beggar in the street (so many of them nowadays), the drunk with the broken leg, the old women who stand in line for hours on end, wooden-faced like totem poles. I saw a boy with Down's syndrome the day before yesterday. I watched him for an hour and felt such warm affection for him for the whole of that time (and, through him, for the whole world). My night fears are me. At a bad moment, when you see yourself in the middle of the night with your swollen eyelids (in the mirror), your eyes bulging from high blood pressure, at a moment like that when you feel like going easy on yourself and showing yourself (at least a bit of) respect, I tell myself my fears are a sign of love. The more love I feel for the downtrodden the more that quivering shred inside me finds peace, that butterfly which is afraid to take flight. (Of course, I know from past experience that nothing special will happen tomorrow, any more than it did at any of the innumerable earlier tribunals. They will question me thoroughly and well, get some point quite clear, find some way of being moderately insulting, and I shall quietly leave.)

It is night (and I have come to a decision).

I needed either to stop thinking about it or just get up and go. I can't sleep in any case, and I have got over my agitation. (So why not do it? A walk at night will be good for my nerves.)

I first got dressed, then carefully turned the key in the door. (I can leave the apartment without having to slam the door.) I took my briefcase with me. Briefcases have had a good effect on janitors in every age, reassuring them as to the respectability of the person before them. A good overcoat, a velveteen cloth cap. (Russian intellectuals have no time for hats and do not wear them. Russian janitors are aware of this.) Actually, there was no pretence. I only needed to dress well, avoiding a casual look. Everything was in place. A small bottle nestled in the briefcase. I looked at the clock: quarter to five. It would take me half an hour on foot. A grey dawn. So what!

The grey dawn proved darker than I had thought, but the air refreshed me, and my legs carried me along smoothly, scarcely recognizable as the heavy night limbs they were only an hour ago. I did not have to hurry.

The four-storey office block stood before me like a dark cube. As I had expected, the janitor was asleep; only he preferred to sleep not at the entrance but somewhere in the bowels of the building, so that my initial tapping and then louder knocking produced no immediate effect. I was about to despair (my plan no longer seeming such a good idea), when I suddenly had the sense to try the windows. I walked along, reaching up and tapping insistently on each of them in turn. A light went on in one of them. The outline of a face pressed against the pane, scrutinizing me. (Each of us looked at the other as if he were a Martian.) The indiscernible face sprang back from the window and disappeared. The old janitor was in no hurry. He took his time getting dressed, possibly went to the toilet on the way. Finally he appeared and de-manded, "Who's that?" The briefcase evidently inspired moderately positive feelings towards me, and he partly opened the door and asked less gruffly, "What is it you're wanting?" with even a suggestion of trust and respect for me (and, of course, for the institution whose safeguarding was his responsibility. In such institutions you don't conduct conversations by shouting at people through the door.).

As I had anticipated, my appearance, the explanation about the important papers I had forgotten, my entirely understandable desire to recover them before the cleaner's arrival, were all wholly convincing. The old man's beady eyes (he was remarkably unshaven and sleepy, but quite possibly no older than myself) probed me one last time and he was persuaded. I drew a blank with the vodka, however. "I don't drink," he said, when I undid the briefcase and pushed it invitingly half open under his nose. I stood there waiting, not closing it again. He snivelled and said, a little stiffly, "A hundred'd be better." He was already going by the new high price for vodka but proposing, as is customary, a discount for cash. I had my wallet on me, and counted him out a hundred roubles.

This unfortunately meant that he would not be staying at his post (sipping an adult beverage from a conveniently sized children's bottle). He would be coming upstairs with the keys and opening the committee room himself. He was quite a bit older than me. (No matter what a person's appearance, you can tell his true age the minute he starts climbing stairs.) We made our way up two flights of stairs before coming to the small meeting chamber. The old janitor opened the door for me. "Go on in. See what you can find. I'll be off back downstairs," a certain tactfulness prompted the old man to say. In a way I had not planned, everything had turned out just the way I wanted. "Fine," I replied. "Some people don't turn the water off at the end of the corridor. They forget to," he complained, listening, as if scanning the whole floor with his ears. It was quiet. No sound of escaping water anywhere.

This may have been only a psychological move on his part, motivated by a desire to make it plain to an outsider that janitors do more than merely keep an eye on a building, and that there are all sorts of other complexities to the job. (People are quite wrong to say that night watchmen get paid for sleeping.) Possibly, however, this was some straightforward practical hieroglyph I did not understand, which implied that I would be going to the end of the corridor for some reason, perhaps to go to the toilet, and should not then leave the tap running. It didn't really matter. He left and went off down the stairs.

And I went in. I went through the door he had opened to me, and now walked round the Table I knew so well, readying myself to take my seat there just as soon as I had fully appreciated it. There were several chairs beside the Table (they seemed to be waiting for their people). Two had been moved back, as if someone had got up abruptly from his place and shoved the chair backwards. Possibly a Young Wolf, I thought. Continuing to move round, I mentally seated them all in their places. I sat on one of the chairs myself. I took a notion to sit, not as the accused but also not as one of the judges. Simply to sit there as of right, saying nothing, and continuing to watch them all in the semi-darkness, trying to work out which of them was which. Then I put the lights on (I was supposed, after all, to be looking for papers I had forgotten) and returned to my seat. I looked for as long as I wanted at the Table and its chairs and laughed softly. I felt a strange influx of power, my feelings were overflowing. I had put my hands palms down (as I had planned) on the Table. I felt I was pressing them down on the baize and the surface of the Table, testing the resistance of the old wood. In a certain agitation I even lightly struck my fist on the Table, "Take that, sirrah!..." enjoying the sensation of the blow. That passed off too without anything happening. But then I reached out for the water decanter, not for a drink; perhaps I just wanted to pick it up. I could not quite reach it, I was just short by the length of a box of matches. I half rose and stretched my hand a bit further forward and then (I remember it was like a whiplash) I felt a tremendous blow in my chest which laid me out for a second or two. I lay, slumped forward on the Table's red baize, my left hand still reaching out for the water.

I did not return to full consciousness, but I was undoubtedly alive. I could hear myself wheezing (all of me, my hoarse breathing, my body, my outstretched arm, lay in the middle of the table. Only my legs were dangling down to the floor. I could feel them somewhere far away.). I was not frightened, and had no other feelings either. Time was a blur, and I do not know how much passed.

The old janitor did not come back, probably having forgotten me or having decided to let me have all the time I wanted for my business. He did not come back until he came upstairs with that early morning cleaner, who immediately ooohed and aaahed and, with the knack elderly women have for identifying and instantly quantifying disaster, pronounced, "He's had a heart attack. As God is my witness, it's a heart attack. Don't touch him. Don't under any circumstances try pulling him!" "Bloody nuisance...," the janitor said irately. "Don't swear." "Why? He can't hear, can he?" "Yes he can." They walked right round not taking their eyes off me, coolly, unhurriedly, as I had myself a while back walked round the Table, sizing it up, appraising it. I might yet fall to the floor. (They discussed just this eventuality with some concern.) My body could slip off the table and go crashing down.

For my part I was conscious of observing, from my state of immobility, the appearance among the many characters with whom I had already mentally peopled the Table of two I had not anticipated: the Teetotal Janitor and the venerable Cardiologist Cleaning Lady. They were involved too. At all events, after due discussion among themselves, they took and implemented a decision affecting my future: they shifted me. (The old janitor carefully raised my dangling legs, and the old cleaning lady caught my shoulders from the other side of the table and pulled me into the middle. At the conclusion of this manoeuvre I was lying fully on the table, rather obliquely but in no danger of falling off.)

The decanter was by my left cheek (close), so that I was mostly on the right-hand section of the table. I heard voices, but these were not yet doctors. It was Them, the people I knew so well.

Out of the corner of my eye I saw the Wise Old Man come slowly over, and with him the Secretarial

Type, and also the former Party Man in his light grey suit. They were talking softly among themselves, already mentioning my name out loud. "Him? Why?" "He had just arrived. No, he isn't first on the list. He had come early." "Was he due to appear today?" The Woman Who Looks Like a Schoolmistress was getting under everyone's feet. She rushed to the door. It was unforgivable, the ambulance taking so long to arrive. It was supposed to be an *emergency* service. "It has only just been called. The janitor didn't have the wits to do it." "Silly old fart!" said the Young Wolf Who Is Dangerous. There were probably some of them standing on the other side of the Table too but my position, lying on my stomach with one arm outstretched and my head twisted to one side, did not allow me to see them. Noticing that my eyes were flickering, some of them moved into my field of vision. They looked at me. I could feel them looking. I moved my lips, trying to smile, to make some pathetic jokey excuse, to say, "Sorry about lying here in the middle of your work place. I'm really very sorry. It just happened. It's all my fault."

Chapter 10

...the Proletarian Firebrand is very pushy (unre-strained). He rattles away as if there were no grammatical cases in Russian. He wants to stifle you at once and only then, when you are buried under a landslide of words (and gasping for air and barely able to breathe), that will be time enough to think about a dialogue. He is strongly prejudiced against intellectuals...

...there is pain in her eyes as if it is not I but she, the Grey-haired Woman in Spectacles, who is at fault (or rather, her son. That is who is at fault, and she bears the responsibility)...

...my daughter... wife... if they are not registered to live in the apartment now it has been privatized...

...the Pretty Woman does not even look at the person being judged. What are they going on about?! (When all anybody thinks about nowadays is money.) She turns away. But she can sometimes suddenly be kind. "Why are you being so mean to him?" she will say suddenly...

...the Secretarial Type is writing, sitting opposite you... the decanter is between you, full of limpid water... you can see your surname arching on a clean sheet of paper (distorted by the curvature of the glass and water, through the decanter)...

...how could you forget? They were all trooping out after some tribunal and one of them, adjusting his scarf, said to another, who was lighting up a cigarette as he walked along, "Yes, of course. You are quite right. It was a completely trivial matter." "What difference does that make? The *client* is dead." They walked on, turning off to the trolleybus stop. (I am a *client*. There is no point in trying to fool myself. It was one of the young ones said it. He smiled, showing off a perfect set of teeth. A Wolf.)

...the Young Wolf Who Is Dangerous usually swings back on his chair while he is speaking. He even rocks on it while eyeing you:

"You think people don't understand you, but people do. People understand you very well indeed!"

He wags his index finger sharply from side to side as if to say, "You aren't going to get away with it that easily, playing hide-and-seek with us, sweetie pie!"

...the Ordinary-looking Woman. She is never the first to start the questioning. She says nothing, but the voracious fires of justice burn in her eyes. (What can you do if people are self-centered, and even your own children are a disappointment? To whom confess your sorrow?)...

...they do it all the time: take everything away (or almost everything) from the person seated in front of them. They take it away and then give it back. Take it away, give it back. They are just being

petty-minded, and markedly different from God who only gives life once and who, if He takes it away, takes it away for good...

...when passions become supercharged those seated at the Table start shouting. The Proletarian Firebrand, that honest drudge, jumps up from his place and leans across the table to get you by the throat: "I recognize you, you bastard. Do you realize, you smug bastard, that the Russian people are slaving away, felling forests with their bare hands!"

...A great pile of papers in front of the little Secretarial Type and Taker of Minutes, a few sheets in front of each one of them, pencils too, stacks – help yourselves. Look, you can take two. Here...